Arise,
Great Lord of the Dead!

"Baron Samedi, hear me!" Maricot chanted.

"I call on you to receive this humble serviteur." She brought the chicken neck to her mouth. "I offer you this sacrifice, Baron Samedi, Baron Cimitière, Great Ghêde, Lord of the Dead."

The circle of people began chanting, rapidly and rhythmically, the batterie maconnique, the mysterious chant that calls the loa, the spirit of dead souls. Maricot waited desperately for a sign, she knew that for this mission no one would do but the Baron Samedi—only he, the god himself, was powerful enough to enter Dorothy, possess her, fire her with a malevolent spirit, and send her back to her father as an instrument of death —*only the Baron could make a killer of her!*

Nightchild

John Meyer

PUBLISHED BY POCKET BOOKS NEW YORK

Another *Original* publication of POCKET BOOKS

POCKET BOOKS, a Simon & Schuster division of
GULF & WESTERN CORPORATION
1230 Avenue of the Americas, New York, N.Y. 10020

ISBN: 978-1-4516-2087-0

First Pocket Books printing September, 1978

Printed in the U.S.A.

For her excellent guide to Voodoo ritual, I am indebted to Maya Deren's *Divine Horsemen: The Living Gods of Haiti*. Dell Publishing Co., 1970.
Also, the contributions of Paul Bartel, David Grossberg, Linda Stewart, and Margaret Whiting must not go unacknowledged.

This book is for Hélène.

smile, exposing yellowed stumps of teeth. She had bled, *bien*. She was of age. He grasped the rattle, the cha-cha, in his weathered fist, offered it to her. Instinctively she shrank from him.

"*Tiens, ma petite, tiens*. You have been chosen." She could not speak, but her eyes asked the question: Chosen? Why? For what? The old man shook the rattle impatiently. It made a sound like a snake. He spoke once more, and the little girl could tell he was very close to death now. In his voice was the sigh of the sepulchre.

"The cha-cha is a talisman . . . a symbol of the power I pass on to you. . . . " He seized her wrist with his bony fingers and pressed the handle of the cha-cha into her hand. Though she dreaded coming into contact with anything the old man had touched, she dared not move. With blazing eyes he burned the phrase into her: "*You . . . have . . . been chosen*." He lay back on his straw pillow and gazed at her for what seemed an endless time. She could not tell when the light went out behind his eyes.

That night the old man was buried in the ocean. There was much drumming and sacrificing of animals and drinking of *clairin*. They placed the pallet aboard a raft big enough to take the whole canopy. By his bed they put melons and rum, clothing and a machete—things he would need in the next world. Also extra food and liquor for Agwé, god of the sea. Then they floated the raft, poured kerosene over it, and set it aflame.

As the raft bucked and hitched its way in the outgoing tide, the little girl watched the black plumes of smoke hiss upward into the moonless sky. The drums and the chanting were very loud now. They would go on all night, she knew, and there would be much dancing and drinking.

She stood on the sandy shore, and as the raft started to dip beneath the waves, she felt something unknown and strange forming within her. The feeling began where she had bled and moved up and around, suffusing her whole body with a peculiar warmth.

By the time the raft sank she knew what the old man had given her.

1

When he saw Raoul at the bar he knew he was in trouble.

"There's your pal," he said to Maricot, across the table.

She didn't stop forking down her pecan pie. "Yes, I ahsked him to meet me here," she said, raising her eyes to the clock on the wall. "I thought we'd hahv talked it all over by now, didn't you?" She put her hand on his arm. "Dahsty," she said, in that voluptuous voice of hers, the voice that had cajoled him into so many things, "we don't have to be spiteful about this, do we?"

"I dunno, baby, really. It's just going to make things harder . . . 'specially on Dorothy."

He glanced over at the bar. Raoul was drinking tomato juice. Not a Bloody Mary, Dusty knew, just plain tomato juice. Raoul was one of those health nuts—no liquor, no smoking, just a lot of working out with the weights, and now and then balling your wife. Dusty had to laugh, Raoul was being so casual, making such an effort not to look at them.

"Dahsty," Maricot said. She was the only girl he knew who had a long U. As if she were from Boston, fachrissake. There was a time he found it endearing. Now it irritated him.

"You and your Edith Evans impressions," he said.

She decided to ignore it. "I hahv to tell you something, Dahsty . . . I'm moving out."

It caught him by surprise. He tried not to show the sudden emptiness he felt in the pit of his stomach. "Yeah? When?"

"Tonight," she said. "While you're in the mountains."

"Beautiful. You and uh—" he gestured to the bar—"Rocco just gonna back the U-Haul up to the apartment and tilt the floor, right?"

A look of tolerance came to her eyes. "I'm only taking what's mine," she said, striking a pose that was her idea of dignity.

"But, Dahsty . . . I want Dorothy."

He stood up angrily. "You can fuckin' go to *hell,* cunt."

Even as the words came out he knew he had spoken loudly, much too loudly, and the late lunch crowd in Joe Allen's paused, almost to a man. Dusty heard the grating of wood on wood as the chairs swiveled around. Every eye in the place was suddenly fixed on their table. Raoul had dropped from his bar stool to the floor in a low, boxer's crouch. Maricot opened her mouth.

Before she could speak, Dusty leaned over, and, as if he were throwing a punch line, said, "And then she slaps his face and the curtain comes down on Act One."

There was an instant laugh of relief from the crowd, followed by a scattering of applause. Dusty picked his coat off the chair, slung it over his arm, and crossed to the door. He turned and looked at her. "Thanks for lunch," he said.

He stopped at the apartment, picked up his tuxedo and the black leatherette case that contained his music. At the door he took a quick survey of the stuff in the room against the time when he would check it, later tonight. Actually, there was nothing he cared about she'd be likely to take. His Fred Allen radio tapes, for instance, his *MAD* magazines (the original, dime-sized ones, complete) —she didn't care about any of that. And he didn't care about the Picasso print (the hands on the flowers) or the Chinese screen in the corner, or the assator, the big drum that hung on the wall. The one thing she would not get was Dorothy.

He got the car out of the garage and drove directly up

to Eighty-ninth and Park. He waited for Dorothy to come through the black iron doors of the Dalton School. Dalton, he thought. I'm living in a shithole on Ninth Avenue and the kid's going to Dalton. Forty-five hundred a year so she can make mudpies with Leontyne Price's kids, U Thant's kids, Bill Cosby's kids. By this time she probably thinks of herself as the token half-caste.

And then she was coming through the big black door, by herself—not in a group, laughing and giggly with the other girls, but by herself. What a loner, he thought, and pressed his lips together. I make her that way, I know I do.

"Dodo—" he called, and she turned, uncertainly, and then spotted him. The little bronze face beamed as she dashed across the street (Watch the traffic, jerko, how many times have we told you?).

She stuck her face in the window, next to his. "Hi, Frankie." Ever since he'd played her Lenny Bruce's Palladium routine she called him Frankie.

"Get in, shweethaht—" (doing his Bogey impression)—"you're coming with me."

Dodo hung back suspiciously. "Where?" she asked.

"Well, shweethaht, it'sh Friday. Where does Frankie always go on Friday?" Dodo began jumping up and down with joy. "The mountains! The mountains!" she screamed. "We're going to the mountains!"

As he swung the Volvo north on the New York Thruway, he knew he'd have to tell Dodo about Maricot sometime during the ride up. By the time they headed home, somewhere between two and three this morning, the kid would be asleep in the back of the car. He was glad he didn't have to drive any singer up with him. Sometimes Leonard asked him to give Betty Rhodes a lift, if she was working the same weekend. Betty was sexy; he'd thought about Betty once or twice, but his loyalty to Maricot always stopped him. Loyalty, man, there was a laugh . . . and for a sorry instant all the missed opportunities with Betty flashed through his mind, along with an ugly frame or two of Maricot making it with Raoul. In our bed, too, he thought righteously, and he knew she had. All those nights I was working in the mountains she was balling Raoul. In our bed.

He glanced over at Dorothy, who was tuning in 99X on

knew anyway. He pressed her little calf once more. "That's okay, Doe—I wouldn't make you tell a secret."

"You have to understand," he told the audience of assorted Jews. "My parents came from the old country." There was a murmur of sympathy. "Carthage." Leonard had warned him not to be too cerebral. "My parents were disappointed in me. They were expecting a child. In fact, after I was born, my mother tried to practice birth control retroactively. I was breast-fed—by my father." He knew it was the wrong material for these people, but he just couldn't bring himself to do crabgrass jokes, Alan King jokes, and his theory was that hipper stuff would work if you couched it in the right syntax.

"My mother confused me. I grew up very confused and disoriented. Show you how disoriented I am, last week I was drowning at Jones Beach, and as I went down for the third time—someone else's whole life flashed before my eyes. Mark Spitz's. Hey, *there's* a *guy*. Where do you girls get to meet a guy like that? Last month I tried one of those computer dating services—" and he was into Computer Dating (What's your favorite magazine? What's your favorite punishment?) and his home-town shtick (I'm from Camden, New Jersey. Pause. There was a time when that meant something.) and his finish (he was so sick of it), "When You're Smiling," with the impressions, eight bars Billy Eckstine, eight bars Vaughn Monroe, bridge Louis Armstrong, and last eight bars Pearl Bailey. A real crowd pleaser. Three bows. Come on back, Dusty. Dusty *Greene*r!

They were sitting in the coffee shop, having a fast hamburger before the drive back. The ladies with the massive bosoms and the men with the white patent loafers passed by with many compliments. Some lingered maliciously, hoping prolonged contact with A Celebrity would afford an opening for a put-down. He ran into this a lot.

"How come ve dun't see you on de TV?"

"They haven't asked me."

"But you're terrific!"

"I know."

Mr. and Mrs. Feinstein, from Great Neck. She with a silver rinse, he with liver spots on his hands.

"You from New York?"

"Yes."

"Vot part?"

"Manhattan." Feinstein still looks quizzical. "Fifty-fifth Street."

"I got a cousin lives in New York, maybe you know him: Bernie Hopper, he's in better coats. But he gets around to all the joints, all the nightclubs."

"No, I'm afraid I don't."

The Feinsteins pause, at a loss for a new topic. They just won't move on—that's how they are, these Feinsteins.

"And who is the young lady, if I may be permitted to ask?"

"Say hello, Doe," Dusty prompts.

Doe smiles. "My name is Dorothy and this is my father."

"Your father?" Mrs. Feinstein registers surprise.

"Sure," says Dusty. "Somebody has to carry on the Greener tradition. Hey, Doe, where you from?"

"The old country—Carthage." The Feinsteins chuckle.

"Hey, Doe—you take a bath today?"

"Why? Is one missing?" Doe wiggles her eyebrows up and down like Groucho.

"Tell me, Dorothy—do you like Kipling?"

"I don't know—" more with the eyebrows. "I've never Kippled."

Mrs. Feinstein beams. "Like father, like daughter," she says.

"You staying here tonight?" This from Mr. Feinstein.

"No, we have to drive back."

"All the way to Manhattan?" Mrs. Feinstein is disturbed. "Why, Dorothy, you won't get to bed before three o'clock in the morning."

"I'm used to it," says Dorothy, but Dusty catches the silent exchange of disapproval that passes between the Feinsteins. Keeps her up till all hours, what kind of father, child won't get to bed till . . . look at the poor thing . . . all she gets to eat is a hamburger in a coffee shop . . . if that were *my* daughter . . .

"Frankie, ask me what I think of the you-know-what-as-a-you-know-what."

Dusty is just pissed off enough to do it. Once, at an impromptu party, Bob Klein had taught Dorothy the old whaddaya-think-of-the-ass-as-a-whole? routine. (Answer: I think it's a dirty crack and oughta be wiped out.)

Dodo takes particular pleasure in mouthing this foul two-liner whenever she gets the chance, and Dusty is tempted now to feed her the setup and let her shock the shit out of the Feinsteins. Except he'd never hear the end of it from Leonard, and he needs these weekends in the mountains. He can do four shows over a Friday–Saturday at two-fifty each—that's a thousand clams (less 10 percent). No, he can't afford to let a story like this get back to Leonard.

He stands up. "C'mon, Doe," he says to his daughter, and "Nice talking to you" to the Feinsteins. The Feinsteins shake their heads.

As they cross the lobby Dusty catches his reflection in the gold-flecked mirror. Not the greatest. The curly hair needs a wash, and the wide, smiling mouth seems glum. Not only that, but the marvelous aquiline Warren Beatty nose is fleshing out under newly acquired weight (it's all this crap-on-the-road food). I look like fuckin' Harpo Marx. On a bad day.

They got home at three fifteen. Dorothy walked like a zombie to the couch and fell on it like a piece of timber.

"Teeth," he said to her, warningly. Dorothy gave a petulant moan of annoyance. "Teeth, Doe, let's go." If he let her, she'd go to sleep on the sofa, clothes and all. He stood there till she realized he meant it, and then she got up and marched into the bathroom, pulling her sweater over her head.

He looked around to see what damage Maricot had done. The first thing he noticed missing was one of the throw pillows from Dodo's hide-a-bed couch. It had been a large needlepoint of an orange rooster, and Doe was fond of it. Okay, fair enough, Maricot had sewn it herself, she was entitled to it.

He went inside the bedroom and slid one of the closet doors open. Yeah, most of the dresses were gone, and the shoes. He slid open the top drawer of her dresser (she had had the whole right side), and it was empty except for one bra, which had a missing hook. He crushed the bra in his hand, struck it fiercely against his leg three times, and impulsively pressed it to his face and took a deep sniff, even as he thought, No, don't do this, don't start with this, watch it. But there it was, the scent of her body—musky, coppery, cunty—and then came the first faint stirrings of an erection. Oh, Dr. Pavlov, here I go, Mr. Proust, taste my madeleine, oh, Christ, shit shit *shit,* and he flung himself angrily face down on the big queen-size mattress, and as the darkness surrounded him he went to her.

Maricot. Dodo called her Apricot. The name was a contraction of Marie-Cocotte. Even from the first, in Haiti, she had been a flirt, learned very early how to attract and manipulate men.

Haitian, yes, the color of strong tea, and so fucking gorgeous that when Dusty first saw her the floor tilted, and he knew the sudden feeling you sometimes get that if you don't possess something your life will turn to ashes.

They were both appearing on the same show, a variety benefit sponsored by the *Daily News.* It was in the ballroom of the Commodore Hotel, and she was one of three backup singers behind a flashy faggot named Paul Hutton, who sported a beard to prove he was butch, and a mixed group behind him to prove he was hip (this was the mid-sixties).

Dusty walked in at two o'clock for rehearsal, and there she was, in jeans and a white turtleneck (would he ever forget), testing the microphone levels with the two other girls. He had to pass them to get to the dressing rooms, and when he did he averted his gaze, deliberately didn't speak to her, though there was ample opportunity. Ordinarily he would've thrown some line, made contact, jabbed her, zinged her, forced her to notice him. But he was scared. She frightened him, which was how he knew he must have her, that she'd become an obsession otherwise. Come on, he kept saying to himself, come on, willya? But he knew something important was happening, and he didn't know why.

He didn't speak to her at all, he kept out of her way, and during the show he watched her from the wing, amazed at how well she moved for a singer. He didn't know it but he was watching native training, island grace. Lithe, sinuous—all those sexy dancer words kept shooting through his mind. Maybe he was talking himself into it. Maybe he was nuts. He turned to the guy standing beside him, a magician (a magician. Christ. These benefits were so corny).

"Hey, am I crazy," he started, "or is that girl—"

The magician waved at him impatiently. "Shut up," he said, and Dusty knew he wasn't crazy. The magician was drooling. He was ready to give up his wife, his career, his everything, and follow her to the Black Hole of Calcutta.

"I'll have to work some magic on *that,*" said the magician, whose name was Mike Imperio.

"Yeah," said Dusty, "make her come out of a hat." And at that moment his desire firmed into resolve. It was the idea of having rivals like Imperio to battle, the idea of challenge, of conquest.

He was on, and he prayed she was watching.

"I'm gonna join the C.I.O. 'cause everyone I see I owe." Oh, God, please, please let her see me working, let her be watching, *please.* It was where he shone, it was where he was in control, where he was at his best, the most himself, the most appealing.

He was doing different impressions then, and when he did Gable that night, or Bogart, he put extra feeling into them, extra sexiness and toughness.

He also did a routine about record album covers, which helped him out with her, inadvertently. The bit dealt with the discrepancy between what was advertised in the liner notes and what was actually on the record. He mentioned a Duke Ellington album, *The Drum Is a Woman.*

"And they got married and had a little set of bongos." It needed to be stronger, but there was the germ of a good hunk in the idea. What the fuck, it was a benefit, he could afford to try out new things.

When the show was over, he casually maneuvered himself next to Paul Hutton in the dressing room. Paul was taking off his pancake base with Albolene cream.

"Hey, Paul, you killed 'em tonight." The singer turned to him, flashing a set of perfect teeth.

"You think so? I thought they were rather sluggish."

"No, wrong, they loved the uh . . . they loved 'Lady Madonna.' " He noticed Paul had really bad skin, like terminal acne, like his face had caught fire and they put him out with a fork.

"Listen, hope you don't mind, I'll tell you what's good for that, Paul—lots of soap and warm water every night before you go to bed." Hutton looked at him strangely. "I'm kidding," Dusty said. "So listen, where do you go from here?"

"We're going to Detroit on Saturday. We have a single coming out and Berry wants us there for some personal appearances."

"Hey, that's terrific." My ass, he thought. You've got a single like I've got inherited wealth. And *Berry,* yet. "Where'll you be staying?"

"We'll be at the Pontchartrain."

My ass. You'll be with somebody's mother.

"So the label is what, Motown?"

"No, Motown is distributing—the label is Java." Paul picked up his makeup case, which was an Avianca flight bag (Mm, thought Dusty, balling Brazilian pilots again), and headed out to join the girls. This was what Dusty was waiting for. He pushed the dressing room door and stood aside, saying deferentially, "After you."

The girls were waiting at the ballroom elevators, and sonofabitch if Mike Imperio wasn't waiting with them. That prick. He had to knock Imperio out of the box right now, otherwise he was gonna come off like just one more schmuck in the long line of suitors for—he didn't even know her name. Imperio was in there pitching, he could see, as he and Paul traveled the long hallway to the elevators. He couldn't make out what the magician was saying, but he saw him laugh, and punch her on the arm in a familiar, buddy-buddy way. Right, it's buddy-buddy, let's pretend we're just pals.

When they were about ten feet away, Dusty quickened his step. Ignoring the girls, he pushed right through the loose semicircle they formed and grabbed Imperio's hand. "Mike! Good to see you! I ran into your wife just the other day and she told me you were gonna be on this show."

Imperio squinted in puzzlement. "You don't know my wife," he said.

Dusty smiled engagingly. "Wait a minute, I'm sorry. Your wife isn't short and blond, is she, kind of Doris Day-looking?" The girls turned to Imperio expectantly, and Dusty knew he'd trapped him. Yes, she is, no, she isn't, it didn't matter—it was the wrong answer. Dusty could feel the hatred pouring from beneath Imperio's eyelids. He wrapped it up. "Ah, no . . . I know who it was. My mistake. But give your little lady my best just the same."

The elevator arrived, and they all stepped in, Dusty

making sure to position himself beside this electric beauty —*that's* what it was, it was energy, it was active, her appeal leaped at you like a jack-in-the-box. As glib as he had been with Imperio, he was at a loss now with the chick. Amazingly, she spoke first.

"I was listening to that routine you did, do you know, about the drahm being a woman?" Her voice was liquid, it was honey, mercury, it had density, texture, oh, Jesus Christ, what am I gonna do?

He said, "Unh-hunh." Brilliant, schmuck.

"It's quite true, you know. Where I come from, in Haiti, the musical instruments do have gender carrotteristics. And the drahm *is* female. One of them is even called the *maman.*" Oh, no, not French, too—he'd always been a sucker for anything French. French was classy, chic, ritzy—Christ, she was still talking.

"—the ogan, on the other hahnd, which is another percussion instrument, is regarded as male."

He couldn't resist it. "We'll have to get together for a jam session," he said, and then he thought, That's right, smartass, talk yourself into the toilet. But she was smiling at him. Maybe she liked that suggestive jock innuendo, maybe she was just panting to give it away. Maybe she thought he was an asshole.

The doors slid open and the whole party fanned into the lobby. Hutton turned toward the Forty-second Street entrance. "Girls," he called, peremptorily.

Dusty gauged the distance with his eyes. They had perhaps thirty feet—two, three minutes and she'd be back in the bunch. Not much time. They were walking behind Hutton and the other girls. Imperio had disappeared.

"Listen," he said to her, and couldn't keep the urgency out of his voice (Cool it, cool it), "what's your name?"

"I am called Marie-cotte."

Mmm, he thought, and I am called Chief Running Nose. "Marie Cutt? Cott? Spell it for me." She smiled and patiently spelled it out. She probably always had to do this. He was ashamed not to be smarter than the other idiots who had to have it spelled out but, damnit, he had to know. They were at the door, about to rejoin Hutton and the others. He put a restraining hand on her arm.

"Now look," he told her, "my name is Dusty Greener, and I want you to remember it, because in exactly one week I'm gonna be calling you on the phone and I don't want to hear you say 'Dusty who?' when I call. Now what's my name?"

She gave him that smile again. Goddamnit. "What's my *name?"* he repeated, harshly.

"Your name is Dahsty Greener," she said, "but if you're calling me in a week, you're going to be calling long distance." The smile widened teasingly.

"Maybe not," he said, and—though it took all his will—he turned and walked quickly through the door.

And the next day he was on the phone to his agent. There were no open dates in Detroit.

"Look, Leonard, I don't care, I'll work the lowest toilet. And for short bread. I'll work the Christian Science Reading Room. I've gotta play Detroit. Now get it for me!"

The best Leonard could do was the Elmwood Casino, in Windsor, just across the Detroit River in Ontario. Will Jordan had canceled out and Leonard was able to book Dusty in for a week, opening for Maggie Whiting.

On the flight out he had a terrible anxiety attack. What if he couldn't find her? What if he found her and blew it? Why was he going through these changes?

The stewardess gave him his earphones, and he listened to a Laura Nyro record and tried to stop thinking about her.

He was overjoyed (and surprised) to find her, as advertised, at the Pontchartrain. Not under her own name, of course, or even Paul Hutton's, but Motown had taken a suite there, for a week. Apparently there was a record distributor convention going on, and there was gonna be a lot of entertaining and partying. He dialed from his room across the river and got a black voice.

"She be back round nahn, you call back then, okay?" And *click*. Gracious crowd. But he suppressed his annoyance, and, at nine fifteen that evening, he called from the pay phone in the hall of the dressing rooms at the Elmwood Casino. The hall smelled of hair spray and nail polish. He had time to identify the odors exactly because it was taking a while for the Pontchartrain operator to put him through, and then a while for the Motown crowd to fetch her. He could hear a lot of laughing and partying going on, and somebody distinctly said, "Dick Clark don't know *shit,*" which cracked him up, and when her voice finally came on the line he almost said, "This is Dick Clark, and I know *plenty,*" but he knew it would only complicate things. She said hello.

"Hi, this is Dusty Greener." There was a startled pause, and he thought, Fantastic, she remembers me. "I toldja I'd call, didn't I?"

"Yes, and I told you it would be long distance."

"Well, surprise, sweetheart, I'm calling from Windsor."

"From where?"

"Windsor, Ontario—we keep it across the river. I'm at the Elmwood Casino, on the bill with Maggie Whiting. My last show is eleven thirty, which means I can pick you up about twelve thirty, quarter to one. What's your room number?"

"Oh, I cahn't tonight. Not possibly." She seemed to consider it. "No, I just cahn't."

He almost asked why not, but wisely thought better of it. Not too eager, not too eager, don't press it . . .

"Well, how's tomorrow? Can you clear it?"

Another pause, then: "Call me about this time—but not here. Call me at Woodward seven, oh-oh-nine-one."

Dusty hurriedly fumbled a pen out of his tux jacket. "Woodward seven, oh-oh-nine-one," he repeated, as he saw Maggie Whiting approach and pass him.

"Guess what," Maggie said, "you're on."

"Yeah?" he shot after her. "How'm I doing?" and he turned back to the phone. It was dead.

He pondered it all night—and all the next day. She'd hung up. Why? Couldn't she talk? Maybe she didn't want to be overheard talking to anyone outside the Motown crowd. She was probably being served up to every two-bit distributor and disc jockey in town. Sure, that was the record biz, all kinds of payola, guys getting two tons of cocaine to plug a record. Listen, a fast bang here and there, that was part of the chick's *job,* man, come on. He hated the thought of her in bed with some of the types he knew in the record biz. Fucking boogie exploiters. Sonsofbitches. Maybe she was Berry's private stock. Berry Gordy himself, the man, the big cheese, prob'ly a fat spade cat with a little dick. Yeah, that was it, the bastard had her reserved for himself. That's why she couldn't get away, she was expected to be on tap for that black motherfucker. Day or night. Anytime. Hi, baby, this is your man, yo' main man, whah don' you jes' wiggle into a taxi an' bring yo' pretty lil ass on ovah? Jesus.

He was suddenly tickled by the whole train of thought, and he started laughing out loud. Wow, he thought, will you look at yourself, will you *look* at yourself.

Through the glass of the Pontchartrain lobby windows he saw her hurrying. *Whoosh,* through the revolving door, and she was beside him in the car.

"I cahn't stay late" were her first words—"I have to be up early for a radio interview."

He raised his hands to a frisk-me position. "Whatever you shay, shweethaht." He had the discouraging feeling that she was just being nice to him, that she really didn't want to see him.

"I was gonna drive out to Bloomfield Hills, but we could have a drink here in the hotel if you want."

"Oh, no . . . I'd rather not. Isn't there someplace nearby?"

He swung out of the Pontchartrain driveway and stopped at the first bar he saw, a place called Harvey's, a singles bar.

As the girl showed them to a booth, Maricot said, "You look different," and somehow her saying that gave him hope. But he was very nervous. He noticed his shirt cuffs had vanished into his sleeves, and he pulled them down. When they were seated he put a cigarette lighter on the table. He didn't smoke, but in case she did, he'd bought a lighter.

"So how's it going?"

"Oh, fine." She blew a geyser of smoke into the air. "You know. You have to play the game."

"What game?"

"Oh, you know. Pretend you're interested in a lot of things you couldn't care less about. Be nice to a lot of people."

Yeah. He knew who that was. "Like who?" he said.

"Well, like this jock tomorrow—" She pronounced it 'Jacques.' "I'm going to hahv to go into a big act. They like you to preen them, you know."

He found he couldn't sit comfortably. Either he had to poise on the edge of the seat, or else he had to sprawl awkwardly, his arm over the back of the booth in a phony position of relaxation.

"Yeah, I guess so. You have to, uh . . . . what do you have to do? Grab their spindle?" Oh, Christ, how could he talk to her? Either it came out smartass gross or tongue-tied schmuck. He couldn't say anything real. It was just awful.

He tried to shake the blind desire that incapacitated his mind. He found he couldn't. It was more than her fantastic body, her provocative manner—much more. And it wasn't just chemistry either, or the love-at-first-sight number he had originally imagined.

There was something uneasy, something practically magic about her. Once you came within her orbit she had you. She threw a kind of force field around you and there was nothing you could do. You were helpless.

He wasn't much more at ease on their second date. They sat in a cocktail lounge in Bloomfield Hills, listening to a pianist sing "Mr. Bojangles." They stayed till closing, and in the car, on the way back to the Pontchartrain (it was about two fifteen in the morning) he debated with himself whether to grab her or not. It was either this time or next time, and he wasn't sure there'd *be* a next time. Still, he didn't want to rush it. She was so . . . enigmatic. He couldn't tell whether she liked him or was just tolerating him. She'd given him no encouragement. Once or twice he'd permitted himself some halfway intimate gesture—sweeping her hair from beneath her coat collar, squeezing her hand crossing the street—and nothing from her. Now, as he pulled up by the Pontchartrain, something inside him said, Get it out, get it into the open, and as she reached for the door he put his hand on her arm.

"Hey," he said. "Let's stop the bullshit."

He saw the look flash across her face. "No, don't worry—I'm not gonna attack you. But, honey, we have to do something . . . I mean, I'm goin' crazy here, I'm not being myself, you're not being yourself, everything is so . . . ah . . . it's forced is what it is. If we have to go through another evening like this, I'll kill myself."

She gazed at him impassively for a moment—and then she did something marvelous, something he'd always remember. It was the real beginning of them, Dusty and Maricot, and whenever he thought of her it was from this moment.

"Dahsty, darling," she cooed to him, sliding toward him on the seat, "stop trying so hard." And she gave him the tiniest kiss, right on the tip of his nose. He was so stunned he barely noticed her slide across the seat and push the car door negligently toward him, just hard enough to let one latch click. Then she was gone.

He drove back through the tunnel in a frenzy, a euphoria. She digs me, he kept repeating, she *digs* me, otherwise why do that, why encourage me? Why bother, unless—he knew she was a prick-teaser, the little bitch, maybe she just wanted, uh, what? What could she possibly want from him? Nothing, he had nothing to give her, she has to mean it, she *has* to.

He threw a dime into the toll-catcher (a dime, wow, was the toll actually a *dime* then?) and he thought, I am the luckiest medium-priced stand-up comic in Windsor, Ontario.

The last time he saw her in Detroit they sat in a coffee shop at the airport and he took her phone number. She was through here, and he had to finish out his week at the Casino.

"But I'm calling you Monday, so save Monday night, willya?" She smiled at him. He knew why she was smiling. Try as he might he could not disguise his eagerness for her.

"I been thinking about us," he continued. "Either we're gonna have the wildest thing of all time, or we'll never see each other again. There's no in between."

"Why cahn't we be friends?" she asked, impishly, and even though he knew she was putting him on, he answered her seriously.

"Fuck that. Who wants to be friends?"

The smile widened. "I know a lot of people who may not *wahnt* to be, but they are."

"Yeah? Well, not me."

The first time they made love together he was so excited to finally possess her that of course he came in three seconds.

"We'll do it again," he gasped. She looked at him with that cool half-smile that could drive him to fury. "We don't hahv to," she said.

But, yes, they did have to. It was a question of Dusty's vanity. He had to prove himself to her, take her, conquer her, break her cool detachment, make her scream with pleasure and rip her nails down his back—the whole macho bit. But when he entered her the second time he felt the same quickening rush to climax invading his loins, and he cursed himself for an incompetent fool—if it wasn't good for her now there might never be a second chance—and he drew his head out of her neck (gaining time, gaining time) and saw her staring at him in the strangest way, the oddest way, as if commanding him, willing him backward, away from the throbbing incontinence that would make him explode and turn to mush in thirty seconds. And it was as if *she* were entering *him* now, through his eyes, somehow she was penetrating his mind, his feelings, with her steady, burning gaze, fixed at a point midway between his pupils, and, yes, the feeling was receding, the irresistible white heat was diminishing, he hadn't stopped thrusting, couldn't stop thrusting, such was his desire for her, but her eyes were glowing with an unearthly message, telling him stop, go back, backward, it was as if—magically—she were in his mind, in his groin, inside his brain, willing his physiological responses, and by God she was succeeding, he subsided, down, down, back, and then he forced himself to stop thrusting (with her help he could do it), and they lay still for a pair of silent, breathing minutes and then, slowly, he began moving inside her again and now it was marvelous, strong and sensual, physical and cerebral, emotional and intellectual. It was simple, it was complex, it was just perfect, terrifyingly perfect, and when they came together he felt her pleasure spread over him so fully, so bountifully, that he knew she was finally his at last.

Minutes later, when he could speak, he said to her, "How did you do that?"

"Mahgic," she replied. "I'm a witch, you know."

"Unh-hunh," he murmured. "You learned in the Orient the secret power to cloud men's minds."

She gave him the smile. "Yes, and aren't you lucky," she said.

He had to admit he was. Whatever she had done, it had worked. Without the aid of her "mahgic" it would all have been over in twenty seconds. But *damn,* it was weird. How could one person do that to another?

He had moved into the apartment on Fifty-fifth Street the year before, and though Maricot would have preferred more opulence, it offered what she called "a chahllenge," and she came to live with him. The one thing she found intolerable, however, was the cockroaches.

"Yeah, I know," Dusty explained. "I've had three different exterminators up here—they just keep comin' back."

"Dahsty, we simply cahn't live like this."

"Well, babe, I dunno what we can do."

He had called yet another exterminator, who came with the big gun and sprayed dutifully behind the fridge and the stove and the sink.

They came home two nights later, and as Dusty flipped on the lights Maricot dashed into the tiny kitchen. "They're back!" she yelled.

"Honey." Dusty sighed. "They're part of living in New York. I wish you'd forget about it." There was silence in the kitchen. After a moment Maricot walked into the living room and sat on the couch. Dusty saw the glint of determination in her eye.

Two days later he came upon a small pincushion on top of her dresser. He had bought her a makeup mirror and rigged a table by the bedroom window, and there, by the mirror, was this strange object. It was fashioned from a length of carrot and a small Spanish onion, the onion joined to the carrot to form a kind of head. Maricot had pierced the body of the carrot with an evil-looking hatpin.

And by that weekend the roaches were gone.

When he asked her about it she told him she cleaned her pins with carrot and onion juice, and by this time he was so in love with her that whatever she told him he wanted to believe. Still, his reason kept returning to . . .

"Daddy, I can't find the cha-cha."

"What?"

"I can't find the cha-cha."

Dusty turned his head, and there was Dodo, standing in the doorway in her undershirt. Past her, in the living room, he could see she'd pulled out the Castro, which made him feel lousy on two counts: one, he hadn't helped her (he didn't care what Bernadette said, the fuckin' thing needed a longshoreman to open), and two, she'd caught him lying face down in Mommy's bra, feeling sorry for himself. He rolled over on his back and beckoned to her. She came and sat on the edge of the bed.

"Did you look in the bookcase?" She nodded. "The toy chest?" She nodded again.

"I looked in the bookcase, in the toy chest, and behind the TV."

With a sigh (he wasn't ready to leave his flashback yet), he shambled into the living room and began searching for the cha-cha. It was this dopey rattle from Haiti Maricot had given her when she was four months old. She always slept with it. Some kids had blankets, Snoopy dolls—Dodo had a cha-cha. It wasn't till he noticed that the assator was gone from the wall that he made the connection.

"Oh, Doe, look, she took the drum. She must've taken the cha-cha, too. We'll call her tomorrow and get it back."

He watched the child climb unwillingly into bed. Thank God she was tired enough not to make a fuss about this. She'd have a right to. He couldn't remember when Doe had gone to bed without the cha-cha. Shit. What a rotten thing for that cunt to do, she knows the kid needs the goddamn thing. What could it possibly mean to Maricot?

He lay naked between the sheets . . . and he couldn't stop thinking about her.

Mendez, Mendola, Mendoza. There he was, Raoul Mendoza, 527 West 23rd Street. Any further west and he'd be in the river, which ain't a bad idea, come to think of it. He dialed the number, a Chelsea exchange. As Raoul picked up on the other end he heard Maricot's voice finish a sentence.

"Speak," said Raoul. Oh, cool, baby, very cool.

"This is Dusty, Raoul. Let me speak to Maricot, please." There was a pause. Dusty pictured Raoul pointing to the phone and mouthing the phrase "It's him." A moment later Maricot was on the line.

"Dahsty, love, I was just going to call you. I wahnt to take Dorothy to Bloomingdale's. She needs a few things. I saw some sweaters on sale—"

"Yeah, well, how about giving the kid back her cha-cha, for openers."

There was a startled pause. "Oh, do I hahv thaht? I don't remember taking it."

"Well, it sure as hell isn't here. We spent half the night looking for it. Poor Doe, she—"

"Let me look for it, and if I come up with it I'll give it to her when she meets me at Bloomingdale's. Why don't you send her over there about three thirty." A tiny warning light began blinking in Dusty's head. Watch it . . . watch it . . . something's up. Remember, this woman isn't yours anymore.

"Listen, Maricot, I have to go over that way anyhow. Why don't I meet you and we'll both do some shopping." He heard her take a moment's pause.

"Oh, Dahsty, you don't want to go through thaaaht, do you? Bloomingdale's on a Sahturday?" She was being very careful not to scare him, not to rouse any suspicion, but it was too late. She was the enemy now, all his instincts warned him, and he had to protect Doe.

"Look, Maricot . . . " He didn't know what to call her anymore—couldn't say honey or darling or Sugardump or any of their private endearments. He had to use her name. "Look, Maricot, if you want to take Dodo shopping, we'll do it together, and that's the way it is. Now, do you want to meet us at Bloomingdale's?"

Another beat. "Dahsty, why are you being so stubborn about this? Really." He smiled.

"You can't kid a kidder, baby." It was tough to stand his ground against her. He was not in the habit of denying her much.

"You're being impossible—you know that, don't you?"

"Yeah, I know that. Tough shit." He was suddenly impatient to be done with the whole thing. If she wanted out, let her go. But nothing bad must happen to the kid.

"What about the cha-cha, Maricot?"

"Dahsty, I'm telling you, I'll look for it, but I don't think we have it." *We,* hunh. So that's how it was now. Okay.

"All right, look for it. I'll call you back in an hour."

When he called back she claimed she didn't have the goddamned thing. Her insistent denials only made him certain she was lying, but there was nothing he could do. Of all the stupid things—a lousy rattle, for Christ's sake.

2

Nothing much changed. The kid was used to Maricot's not being there (it was almost like old times). When he didn't take the kid with him on a job, Gina from next door baby-sat till one, maybe two in the morning.

The goddamned Con Ed bill was forty-eight bucks for August, and now it was mid-September and still hot as hell. School was starting again Monday, and Dodo was hoping against hope she wouldn't get Miss Ross for homeroom teacher.

"Why, Doe?" He was thumbing through *TV Guide,* marking off the movies. *Ziegfeld Follies* was on Thursday night, late, with Red Skelton's "Guzzler's Gin" routine, and a Fanny Brice sketch, both of which he wanted to tape. He left his cassette machine by the set, and occasionally he could pick up good ideas for hunks, and voices to mimic, and material from other comics.

Doe was sewing a patch on her oldest jeans. She'd learned to sew from one of the kids in school (Think Maricot would ever teach her? Forget it). But she looked very pained.

"Rossie picks on me all the time. All the time. And Marvin never says anything."

"Who's Marvin? And what color is he?"

"Marvin Berman—his father's writing a book on vowel sounds. And we do homework together, and, you know, mess around, and half the time it's him who's, you know, making noise and everything. But Rossie never picks on *him.*"

"You need some new jeans?"

"No, I'm just, you know, decorating these."

"Where did we get those?"

"Korvettes. They're fine. I'm just, you know—"

"Decorating them, I know. When did you start saying 'you know' all of a sudden?"

Dodo looked at him with a puzzled grin. "I always say it."

"Well, you can cut it out. It sounds rotten and it's not economical."

"Economical?" The little eyebrows went to the ceiling.

"That's right. It gets in the way of what you're saying, it holds up your premise. Suppose I said to the audience 'my parents came from, you know, the old country.' " Dodo began concentrating very seriously on the patch. "You see what I mean, Doe? Sounds bad, gets in the way." Dodo made some noncommittal noise.

"Yeah, these are from Korvettes, I think," she said. She made a big deal of biting off the thread. "Hey, Frankie, could I get some custom jeans? I saw this ad in the *Village Voice* for, you know, jeans they—"

"What did I just get through telling you?"

"—for jeans they custom-make to your body," Doe corrected herself. "They're thirty-five dollars."

"Oh, right, I'm just about to spring for a fast thirty-five bucks so you can outgrow special jeans by next fall. Right. I'll take a cab."

Chastened, Dodo began carefully testing the patch for any possible imperfection or weakness. He watched her for a moment. She was such a good kid, and he came down on her so heavy sometimes. It really wasn't necessary. She idolized him. The slightest word of anger from him and—though she tried not to let him see it—she dissolved.

"You know why Rossie picks on you, don't you, Doe?" His voice was softer now. Doe glanced up at him.

"Why?"

" 'Cause she knows you're the smartest. She knows you can take it."

Doe made a face. "Yeah, well, thanks a lot," she said.

He stood in the dim hallway, by the row of letter boxes, and stared at the envelope. In the top left corner it said CIVIL COURT OF THE CITY OF NEW YORK, COUNTY OF NEW YORK, and when he opened it he saw the word SUMMONS in Gothic script, and beneath that he saw his name, and beneath that,

> WRIT OF HABEAS CORPUS FOR CUSTODY OF CHILD
> The people of the State of New York.
> TO DUSTY GREENER aka BENJAMIN GREENBERG, Defendant.

> WE COMMAND YOU that you have the body of Dorothy Greenberg by you imprisoned and detained, as it is said, together with the time and cause of such imprisonment and detention, by whatsoever name the said Dorothy Greenberg is called or charged, before the Supreme Court of the State of New York, at a special term, Part 5 thereof, appointed to be held in and for the County of New York, at the Courthouse, 60 Centre Street in the City of New York on the 4th day of October at 10 o'clock in the forenoon of the said day, to do and receive what shall then and there be considered concerning him, and have you then and there this writ.

And at the bottom it was witnessed by a judge.

Just try it, he thought, just you try it. He marched out of the building, out of the cool of the lobby into the scorching September heat. The surly, glowering kids were playing handball against the walls. Shit, even this heat didn't stop them. He stepped into the phone booth at the corner of Fifty-fifth and Ninth, and thumbed through the frayed directory for Mendoza.

"Speak." Yeah, right, count on Raoul.

"This is Dusty, Raoul, lemme speak to Maricot." There was a muffled instant as Raoul placed his hand over the receiver. Someday, weights or no weights, I'm gonna beat the shit out of that motherfucker.

"She says, 'Whaddaya want?' "

"What do I *want?* I want to know how come I got a custody notice in the mail, that's what I want."

"Yeah, that's right, you got a notice. So do what it says."

"Look, Raoul, you want to put my wife on, please?"

Another muffled pause. Then: "She says she got nothing to say to you, man. She'll see you on the fourth." And *click.*

During the creaky elevator ride back upstairs he stuffed the summons into his pocket. The important thing was Dodo—how could he tell her about this? Up to now Doe thought Maricot was just taking some kind of extended vacation, and he let her think so. It was easier on her this way. But if Maricot insisted on this stupidass custody suit, Doe would be caught in the cross fire. He knocked on the door of 5C and Mrs. Antonucci opened up.

"Hi, Mrs. Antonucci—just wanted to remind Gina about tonight." He crossed the hall as he spoke, to 5B, his apartment. He didn't want to get caught in a lengthy (and boring) reminiscence of Rome in the fifties, which is what would happen if he allowed Mrs. Antonucci to draw him into conversation. He just wanted to make sure Gina would be over to stay with Dorothy that night.

"Oh, she doesn't forget, Mr. Greener—she looks forward to it. Even when she was a little girl, in Rome—"

"Thank you, Mrs. Antonucci, then we'll see her about six fifteen." There was a lot to think about, and he welcomed the solitary drive to—where was it tonight? Long Branch, New Jersey. The Harbor Island Spa. An hour and a half. Time to think.

3

He didn't play the radio on the drive down. All right, he thought, I'm gonna hafta get a lawyer. Jesus, who do I know? And what's it gonna cost me? Can you answer a summons yourself?

At the entrance to the turnpike the machine whirred the ticket from its maw like a kid sticking out her tongue. Instead of rejoining the turnpike traffic Dusty steered the Volvo to the side, where the trucks did their sleeping. He reached back to his suede jacket and pulled the summons out again.

When you reduced the legal jargon, all it said—basically—was have the kid there and bring this paper. No charge was mentioned, no action of any kind. Just bring the kid and the paper. Dusty put the car in first and whipped back onto the highway. Maybe this was just harassment, just Maricot and Raoul being nasty—Let's get him down there, make him waste a few afternoons. But deep in his bones he knew she meant to take his kid away.

He got to Long Branch at quarter to six. Music rehearsal was called for four, but he knew the singer, whoever she was, would take an hour and a half, minimum.

He'd worked the Spa before, he was familiar with this band. Anyway, all he needed from them was one fast chorus of "When You're Smiling," which they could play in their sleep. And usually do, he thought, as he schlepped his clothes and music across the lobby. Lenny, the social director, was setting up an art auction. These hotels always had something going on: tennis, chess, badminton, backgammon—whatever. Tonight it was an art auction. Christ, what crummy paintings—at least five magazine-illustration chicks with taffy hair and limpid, innocent/provocative eyes, framed in heavy gold. At least eight Paris street scenes (in the rain, of course) done in little dots. This shit would go for three, four hundred dollars after dinner, when people like the Feinsteins were feeling expansive.

"They're waiting for you, Dusty."

As Dusty opened the doors to the dining room a Marty Balsam type in tennis shorts and a Lacoste shirt puffed by behind him. They all wanna win the Davis Cup, at age fifty-five, he thought as he entered the room.

"Hiya, Tommy," he said to the piano man. "Oh, shit, you're not growing a beard! I can see the Cream of Wheat dripping off it right now." The other four guys broke up. "You look like Fu Manchu—just before he died."

"Just *after* he died," put in Gary, the drummer.

"*Long* after he died." Dusty put the capper on it and took a friendly swipe at Tommy's chin.

Tommy shook his head resignedly—he had been getting a lot of this. "You turkey," he said.

It was good relations to kid around with the band. A happy band played better, and they remembered you. You never knew when a Vikki Carr was gonna need someone to open the bill for her, and someday, somewhere, Tommy would be playing piano for Vikki Carr. Dusty gave Tommy the piano conductor book, and passed out the others—bass, drum, trumpet, sax.

"Okay, Tommy, remember this? Just gimme tempo under the talk. Cue line is 'and none of us're getting any younger.' "

" 'When you're smiling—' " Dusty sang. The trumpet and the saxophone gave two short stings, *bwap-bwap*.

" 'When you're smiling (*bwap-bwap*)

" 'The whole world smiles with you . . . ' " And he was into the song, very softly, merely mouthing the lyric and keeping time as he let Tommy and the guys do a chorus

Thank you, Dr. Krankheit. Dusty smiled. What if one of those interns had come on like Smith and Dale. Dynamite. He heard a voice in the lobby say, "I think he's in there," and a moment later he saw Mrs. Slotkin in the doorway of the lounge. She looked very agitated.

"There you are," she said. He rose as she came to him. "I have to go with my husband," she said, "but I couldn't leave without thanking you. You probably saved his life."

She had a strong New York accent, but her manner was brisk and precise—better than most of these Feinsteins. Kind of a yenta Nina Foch.

"Did the doctor say that?" Dusty asked.

Mrs. Slotkin made a pooh-poohing motion with her hand. *"I'm* saying that. I know you saved mine. If Gerry had just been lying there, in agony, without anyone to help him, it would've been more than I could bear." She paused, and Dusty saw tears spring to her eyes. "I honestly don't know how to thank you."

"Forget it," he said. Yeah. Tough guy. He had to stop playing these roles. Too many Bogart impressions.

"No, I won't forget it. Listen, I have to go to the hospital—"

"Is there a good one around here?"

"Yes, Monmouth Medical Center, it's not far. Now, Dusty, I want you to promise me something: promise you'll call me Monday at this number." She gave him a business card and turned to go. He took her arm.

"It's really not necessary," he said.

"It is for me. Now promise me, Dusty—" Who was she, fachrissake, his mother?

"All right, already, I promise. Now what else can I do for you?" As she left the lounge, he broke up for perhaps the fiftieth time that evening. Now he had to call the widow Monday. He chugged the rest of the Dubonnet.

He was still chortling as he put his clothes and music in the back seat. Wait till Leonard hears this. He'll be able to raise my price. For medical services. He put the Volvo in first. That's me, he thought: Dusty Greener, Songs, Clever Patter, and Mouth-to-Mouth Resuscitation.

He didn't look at the card till he got home. As he was emptying his pockets he felt the sharp edge go under his thumbnail. As if to remind him. Annoyed, he threw the card on the dresser with his wallet, bills, and keys. It was a classy card, of that springy, parchmenty stuff, with elegant, raised navy blue letters:

ARLINE SLOTKIN
Attorney
The Legal Aid Society
80 Lafayette St. CH 4–4200

The first thing he asked Mrs. Slotkin on Monday was, How's Gerry?

"He's okay, considering. Has to stay quiet, of course. But he's really anxious to meet you."

"*Meet* me? We're practically engaged."

"He doesn't remember much about the other night. Listen, Dusty, in about three weeks I want to give you a party. I have a friend, Mal Kishnevsky, maybe you know him?"

"I don't think so, Mrs. Slotkin."

"He's in publicity, handles a lot of show people, I thought you might know him. Anyway, I know he can do something for you. So at this party—"

"Mrs. Slotkin, hold on." He had met enough Mal Kishnevskys through enough Arline Slotkins to know it was a waste of time. "It's very kind of you, but lemme take a pass on it, please."

Arline Slotkin's voice got almost panicky. "Dusty, you've got to let me do this for you."

Dusty had been thinking about it. Now he said: "Look, Mrs. Slotkin, you really wanna do something for me? I mean, is this some kind of, aah, cross you're gonna walk around with for all time unless you—"

"Dusty, you saved Gerry's life."

"Okay, then, I tell you what. I notice you're an attorney, right?"

"Yes, for the Legal Aid Society." Her voice became concerned. "Are you in some kind of trouble?"

"Who knows? No, I wouldn't call it trouble. I have to answer a summons."

"What kind of summons?"

"Well, I have a ten-year-old kid, a little girl, and her mother and I, we're separated, and I got a summons from her ordering me to bring Dorothy downtown. Sixty Centre Street. So my question is, what the fuck do I do? Pardon my French."

Suddenly Mrs. Slotkin was all business. "What's the date on the summons?"

"October fourth."

There was a brief pause, while Mrs. Slotkin did some figuring. Then she said, "I'll be there. Now listen to me. There's a coffee shop on Lafayette Street, next to the courthouse. I want you to meet me there at nine thirty in the morning on the fourth. Can you do that?"

"But *natürlich,*" said Dusty, with a faint German accent. "Look for a man viss a thin scar, chust above the eyebrow. He vill pe carrying a volume of Henny Younkman's vun-liners." He knew he was being a jerk. Whenever he was faced with the unpleasant realities of life he protected himself with this kind of tummeling, shticks, bits, dialogue from old Buster Crabbe movies. He'd done it with Gerry's heart attack. Now he was doing it with his court case.

"I'm sorry, Mrs. Slotkin, I'm just being an idiot. This is more than I expected. You really don't have to—"

"The coffee shop, Dusty. Nine thirty."

"I got it. I'll see you there. And thanks, I mean really, thanks, and uh . . . tell Gerry I miss him, will you?"

"I will, Dusty. And do yourself a favor: don't discuss this action with anyone."

"Why not?"

"Just don't."

It was the Monterey Coffee Shop on Lafayette Street, across from the Family Court Building.

"Why do I have to sit at the counter?" Dodo wanted to know.

"Because Mrs. Slotkin and I are talking about you, Schmucko, and we don't want your head to swell up like a balloon."

"Yes?" said the counter girl.

"Whaddaya want, Doe? How about an English muffin and some hot chocolate?"

"Do you have corn muffins?" Doe asked. "*Ang*ela," she

enunciated carefully, staring widely at the octagonal name tag the girl was wearing on her shoulder. What a flirt. Watch out, world, here comes Dodo.

"Toast me a corn, Eggie," Angela cried back. *Eggie.* Jesus.

He sat down at one of the tables, across from Mrs. Slotkin. As soon as he put his arm on it, the table listed toward him, away from Mrs. Slotkin. They exchanged one of those this-is-how-it-is-in-New-York looks, and he said to her, "How's Gerry?"

"Much better. Walking. Let me see the summons." He handed it to her and she scanned it quickly, then tossed it back across the table.

"How long were you married to this woman?"

"Ten years. We're still married. We're separated. She moved out a month ago."

"Are you planning to get divorced?"

Something inside him tightened at the idea. Even now, after a month, he had trouble accepting it. Divorce. Ten years of his life. Maricot, the magnificent Maricot, so warm, so giving, eager for adventure, impatient for life to shower itself on them. What changed it all?

"Because if you are, this question of Dorothy should be part of the divorce action."

No, he decided. No divorce. If she's gonna act this way, fuck her. "No, I'm not gonna divorce her, Mrs. Slotkin. Let her sweat for it." He caught himself being vindictive. "Look, we don't need to get into that. Let's concentrate on the kid." Automatically, reflexively, he twisted around to check on Dorothy.

"Dusty, have you ever tried sitting perfectly still for one moment?"

Dusty looked at Mrs. Slotkin quizzically. "Why?"

"Just curious. Since we sat down here, you've bitten off a piece of skin from your thumb, you've rearranged the ash tray and the sugar shaker, and all through this your foot's been jiggling up and down like crazy. I just wondered if you ever sat still."

"No. I never do. My whole life is lived like there's a cab downstairs with the meter running."

She gazed at him reflectively. "All right, Dusty, I'll tell you what you can do: you can bring a neglect action against your wife for desertion, adultery, whatever, and if you win, the court'll award you placement."

"What's that?"

"You get to keep Dorothy for a specified time; usually two years. At the end of two years the case is reviewed for extension."

Dusty winced involuntarily. "That sucks. I want her forever."

Mrs. Slotkin shook her head. "Well, Dusty, in that case you'll have to bring a countersuit of your own to win permanent custody."

Dusty slapped his palm on the table with a sharp rap. "That's it! I'll take it," he cried. "Gimme two of those. You got it in other colors?"

Mrs. Slotkin smiled. "Dustele, you don't leave till it fits." Dusty gave Mrs. Slotkin a look of appraisal.

"Hey, Mrs. S.," he said, "you're pretty fast—for a girl." Mrs. Slotkin rose from the table.

"Call me Arline, why don't you?" she said.

Outside the courtroom people were huddled in knots of two or three. As he held the door for Mrs. S., Dusty heard an old lady say to her lawyer, "That don't matter to me," and he wondered what it was that didn't matter so to this fierce, tattered survivor. "Go ahead, Doe," he said, scooting the kid before him with an impatient three flicks of his wrist. The doors swung shut behind them and they were in the large room with the high ceiling. Lining the benches were more old ladies, hookers, delinquents (a lot of delinquents—Spanish or black teen-agers with quick, darting, sullen eyes).

And then he saw Maricot. She was sitting at the end of the third row, looking simultaneously demure and seductive in a beige knit dress with a big, floppy, neckbrace-style collar. His heart started going, as it always did when he saw her. He pulled Mrs. S. closer to him and hissed in her ear. "Ya see the chick in the clinging dress? That's her."

The kid squeezed his hand. "Should I say hello?"

"Not yet, Dorothy," Mrs. S. said. "Let's see which way the wind is blowing." She indicated the last row, and Dodo obediently took the third seat in. Mrs. S. had seen something at the front of the room. "Well, well, well," she said, sitting next to Dusty, "look who we have here. Lytell Everett." Dusty followed her gaze to the bailiff's corner.

The bailiff's head was down and he was listening intently to a lot of expensive tailoring.

"What's a Lytell Everett?"

"A very high-powered attorney, the F. Lee Bailey of divorce."

Dusty's lips parted in fascination as the man in the Church shoes and the Sulka shirt crossed the floor confidently to Maricot, bent with a dancer's grace to her ear, lingered long enough to speak a brief sentence (his eyes fixed on the back of the room), and then, with long, buoyant strides, virtually glided out through the double doors of the courtroom. Everyone swiveled to note this elegant passage.

Dusty rolled his eyes. "I think there's an opening in the Joffrey," he muttered.

"Don't let the walk fool you, Dusty. This is a very sharp cookie. And an expensive one. Your wife must've latched onto some big money."

No, sweetheart, Dusty thought, not money. Maricot deals in a much more potent currency. He wondered fleetingly how Maricot had put herself in a position to meet a man like Everett. He had seen men approach her in restaurants, department stores, any public place. Maricot dug hanging out in expensive shops (Mark Cross, Hermes) and restaurants (21, La Caravelle). If it had been a restaurant, Raoul would've been along as escort. Poor Raoul, Dusty thought, looking at the guy sitting next to Maricot in the third row; how do you stick a cigarette pack under the sleeve of a suit jacket?

The judge came in, and everyone had to stand.

"Blanchard," Mrs. S. whispered. "Good. He's liberal."

I don't care if he voted for Eva Braun, Dusty thought. Just let him give me my kid.

Mrs. S. was sure Everett's conversation with the bailiff had been for the purpose of getting their case called quickly, but, notwithstanding the lawyer's vaunted influence, at four fifteen P.M. *Greener* v. *Greener* had not been called.

"See what I mean?" Mrs. S. said to Dusty. "That's Blanchard. Never mind the high-powered names, with Blanchard you wait your turn."

"Like the chicks with Sinatra," Doe piped up.

"What, dear?"

"That's why Sinatra never gets lay," Doe continued calmly.

"*Laid,*" Dusty corrected her. "And we don't use that word in public."

Dodo pretended not to hear. "All the girls say to him, 'Just because you're Frank Sinatra, don't think I'm going to bed with you.' That's how Judge Blanchard is, right?"

Mrs. S. smiled, and Dusty shook his head in resignation. Doe loved using all the grown-up words. She had no idea what any of them meant.

"Greenberg, Benjamin. Benjamin Greenberg." The bailiff bellowed it from behind the railing. "Greenberg, Mary Coat."

"That's us," Mrs. S. said as they rose to their feet.

"C'mon, Doe." Dusty took her hand and the three of them moved up the center aisle to the railing, where the bailiff drew the velvet rope aside and allowed them to take their places in front of the long table that stood before the raised judicial bench. Dusty glanced over at Maricot but she kept her eyes steadfastly on Blanchard's face. You cunt, he thought, you're even working the judge. But Blanchard seemed impassive.

"Counsel may approach the bench," he said.

Mrs. S. and Everett swung around opposite sides of the table and stopped before the judicial fortress. They began speaking in undertones, and Dusty strained to hear what was being said. He could only catch a phrase here and there: " . . . . ten, ten years old . . . separated . . . presently with her father . . . asking total custody. . . . " Dusty saw Blanchard's eyes flick once to Dorothy. He did not look at either Dusty or Maricot.

Then Everett took a step away from the bench and said (loud enough for all to hear), "Your honor, this case is obviously too complex to begin today, with less than an hour of court time remaining. I move for an adjournment to the twelfth." He looked at Mrs. S. "If that's convenient for everyone," he added. Dusty figured rapidly —this was Tuesday the fourth; the twelfth would be a week from tomorrow, Wednesday. That was okay, as long as it wasn't a Friday or Saturday when he might have a couple hours' drive to make. Mrs. S. looked at him and he nodded his assent. Shit, he thought, this is gonna take forever.

4

They were home, the two of them. It was about ten past seven. He was going to cook scaloppine for dinner.

"Doe, come in here and scrape the carrots, willya?" he called to her.

She was lying on the living room floor reading *The Monkees Fan Letter* and listening to 99X. "Aaaawwww," she said.

"And then you can set up the recorder."

"Who's on?"

"Winters. Channel four. Eight o'clock."

Doe made a face. "I don't think he's funny. I think he's retarded."

"Right. Dodo Greener, noted authority on American humor, claims Jonathan Winters, one of comedy's leading practitioners—"

"He is. He's retarded."

Dusty unfolded the scaloppine and set it aside on the chopping board. He smoothed out the thick butcher paper and spread down a layer of flour. He sprinkled salt and pepper into the flour, mixed it with his finger, and began to dredge the tissue-thin slices of veal. They were too thin. Shit, he thought, I made such a point of having them pounded, they're goddamned nonexistent. See-through scaloppine. He looked into the living room and thought, The kid is reading that stupid rag again.

"Hey, Doe, did you hear me?" He put a little edge in his voice and it got Doe to her knees, at least, and took her head out of the fan magazine. The deal was this: for every forty-five minutes of homework completed, she got fifteen minutes of *Crawdaddy* (or *TV Mirror* or *David Cassidy at Yale* or whatever). Ninety percent of her time was spent keeping track of the groups. Led Zeppelin was in, the Stones were in. The Bay City Rollers were out. Dr. Buzzard might be coming back. This kind of news was exchanged nightly on the phone (but only after *all* the homework was done) by the kid and Marvin Berman.

Doe joined him in the kitchen, got the cook's knife out of the drawer, and started cutting the tops and tails off the carrots.

"I bet I could kill someone with this," she said, and giggled. "I bet I could kill Marvin with this. He is a real *re*tard."

"Yeah? Why?"

"He told me this really retarded thing. He told me about sex intercourse."

"Sexual intercourse." Dusty kept his eyes on the dredging. "What'd he tell you?"

"He said when you and Mommy had me you put your penie in her hole and then you . . . you know."

"No, I don't know. What'd I do?" He was stacking the veal now, in a neat pile. Six pieces.

"You know. You peed in her."

Dusty blew a *pfffft* of disgust through his lips. "That's what Marvin told you, hunh?"

"Yeah. I told him he was crazy, right, Frankie? I told him he was just a *re*tard."

A fierce anger welled up in Dusty as he heard the anxiety in Dodo's tone. That fuckin' Marvin! Yet he knew there was no sense blaming Marvin—it had to come sometime, from somewhere. Actually, Marvin had come pretty close. Closer than a lot of the bullshit *he'd* heard at ten. He remembered, "My Bonnie lies over the ocean/ My Bonnie lies over the sea/ My father lies top o' my mother/ And that's how they got little me." Not too much hard information there, right? Now she was *ask*ing, she was giving him the setups. All he had to do was throw the punch lines. Do it right, putz, he told himself.

He looked at her. She had cut the carrots in thirds and then cut the fat thirds in half, as he'd taught her, so the pieces would be the same size (Why? she'd asked. So they'll cook evenly, he'd explained). Now she was placing the carrots in boiling water, taking care not to splash any on her little hands. He could feel her holding her breath, waiting for him.

"All right, honey, now first of all, what are the proper names? It's not the penie, it's the—" He held out his palm.

"Penis," she gave him.

"Right. And it's not the hole, it's the—"

"Vagina."

"Right. And the baby grows where?"

"In the mommy's belly."

"Right. And what do we call that?" Pause. "Where the baby grows?"

She frowned in a parody of concentration. "I forget."

"Starts with a W."

"The wang?"

Christ. From Dalton, yet. More giggling now. "C'mon, schmucko."

"I forget."

"The womb, remember?"

"Oh, yeah! The womb. And the baby is an egg—now I remember. But I still don't understand . . . ummm . . . " She was hooked now, but shy—embarrassed at not knowing, at the hazy sense that the whole business was somehow, umm, you know . . . dirty. Christ, he was trying so hard to keep the lines open.

"Don't understand what, Doe?"

"Ummm . . . how the egg gets into the, ummm . . how it . . . you told me there was an egg every month."

"That's right. And if it doesn't get fertilized by the daddy it drops out."

"Really?" Eyes widening. A little nervous.

"Yep. Which reminds me," (it was an opening he'd been looking for,) "you'll start making eggs pretty soon, baby, and they'll start dropping out, and I don't want you to be scared when you drop that first egg, Kiddo, 'cause sometimes if you don't know what's happening, you can get frightened."

"Why?"

"Well, there's a little blood. And that's why Mommy wears those things—you remember those things Mommy used to put inside her, those Tampaxes?"

"Unh-hunh."

"Well, that was to soak up the blood from the egg, you dig?"

Doe made a grimace of distaste. "Am I gonna smell like that? Like Mommy did?"

Christ, don't remind me, he thought, you'll get me hot. "Sure. Everybody does. And you know what? A lot of people like it."

Doe wrinkled her nose. "Yuccchh. That's retarded."

He reached across her as casually as he could (Stay cool, stay cool), and dropped a half a stick of butter into the skillet. The yellow oblong began to sink into the pan, spreading a thick circle of syrup outward. He could feel her thinking.

"Does the Tampax hurt when you put it in?"

"No, honey."

"Does the baby hurt when it comes out?"

"No, honey." Tell her the truth. "Oh, maybe a little. Not for long."

"But the baby's so big, and the vagina is . . . just . . . " The sentence trailed off. Finish it, finish it, baby.

"But what happens, Doe? To the vagina."

"It stretches. But doesn't *that* hurt?"

"There are exercises you do while you're pregnant. Mommy did them, and someday, when you want to have a baby, you can do them, too."

"Does exercise make the vagina bigger?"

"No, honey, just more supple, more limber, you know?"

"You're not supposed to say 'you know,' you know," she said with a big straight face.

"I know," he said, as the carrots boiled, and the butter started popping, and he had to grab her up in his arms so she wouldn't see the tears springing down his cheeks.

5

"—and on the basis of this evidence—" Everett was chanting, "we intend to *show*, clearly and *graph*ically, that the life this child leads with her father is detri*mental*—not only to her health and physical well-being—" (pause) "but to her e*mot*ional growth and development as a *mature young woman*."

He ends his sentences on the upbeat, Dusty was thinking, and you wanna applaud. He can say anything, it's an applause getter. And we will take you *outside* (pause) and *chop off your balls*. Yayyy!

Everett pointed a manicured finger at Dusty. "This *child*" (pause) "lives with a *father*" (pause) "whose prime concern is his career as a *nightclub comedian*. The man is absent from the house three nights a week, sometimes more." (pause) "Three . . . nights . . . a *week*." Everett emphasized this phrase by striking his gold-filled pen against the yellow pad he was holding.

"And *worse* . . . when Mr. Greener *does* see fit to attend to his child" (pause) "he compels her to follow the same far-from-healthy routine *he* is forced to observe by the exigencies of his business." (long pause) "We intend to show that this child is constantly *kept awake* until *three o'clock* in the morning," (pause) "that her eating habits are ir*reg*ular and un*heal*thy," (pause) "that her home life in *no way* approximates the stable environment in which a child *should be raised*."

Everett was an effective performer—he never looked at the judge, never became a supplicant for attention. Dusty had learned this lesson in comedy. You look over their heads, you zing the punch lines into the ceiling, into the floor, and sometimes (with eyes closed) into yourself. Then they affirmed you with laughter, and you could look at them. Except there're no laughs in a courtroom, Booby. Everett was winding up. His opening remarks had taken over half an hour. Now he moved to the chair at the end of the long table and pointed to Maricot. "This child," he said, "belongs with her mother." And he sat down, placing the pad in his lap.

They were in the Family Court on Centre Street. This was not a jury trial, it was a private hearing, in closed chambers. The only people present were the principals, their attorneys, and the witnesses who had been subpoenaed to give testimony. Dusty recognized Maricot's friend Syndee Lawrence (her stage name), a fellow dancer and a real looker (good-looking girls ran together). She was dressed down for the occasion in a demure slacks and sweater outfit covered by a blue blazer (he could hear Everett's words—Don't look flashy).

Mrs. S. was standing before the bench. Blanchard looked down at her. "Does defense wish to make an opening statement?" he asked.

"Judge," said Mrs. S., "it's never very pleasant to plead a case based on the destruction of a person's character—yet that is precisely what Mrs. Greener is forcing Mr. Greener to do, through this spiteful and unwarranted action. Unless Mrs. Greener is willing to drop this suit for custody and leave the defendant, Mr. Greener, in peace, we are prepared to show that she, and not Mr. Greener, is the culpable party in the matter of parental responsibility. We will cite evidence to prove that she is, first, an adulteress, a woman who willfully left her home, husband, and child for the bed of another man, second, a user of drugs—and by drugs I mean hard drugs, not marijuana—and third, a mother whose principal interest, far from raising her child in a loving and stable environment, is only her own selfish pleasure and position in a milieu totally unrelated to that of motherhood."

Holy shit, Dusty thought, she's gonna blow 'em through the roof. And indeed Mrs. S. had produced a tension, a crackle of electricity, in the air. Blanchard was leaning forward over the bench. Now Mrs. S. turned to Everett.

"Mr. Everett, do you truly wish to associate yourself with this case?"

From his seat at the table Everett lifted a casual finger.

"Objection. Judge, would you explain to counsel that I am not on trial here?"

"Sustained," said Blanchard. "Counsel will confine her questions to the witnesses. Have you concluded your opening remarks, Mrs. Slotkin?"

"Yes, Judge." said Mrs. S. and resumed her seat.

"We have roughly three quarters of an hour, Mr. Everett. Do you wish to call a witness?"

"I do, Your Honor," said Everett, rising. "I call Mrs. Benjamin Greener to the stand."

As Maricot walked calmly, almost sedately to the witness box, Dusty was sure this was part of Everett's direction, too. Normally, with her energy and enthusiasm, Maricot never *walked* anywhere. She jiggled, she pounced, she bounced. He had seen her bounce from the chair to the couch, hop from the kitchen to the bedroom—it was part of her, the way she moved, one of the sexiest, most attractive parts of her—and suddenly he knew why she was walking this way, so deliberate, so klutzy: Everett didn't want her coming off even remotely seductive. Actually, there was no way of toning down the basic appeal. Even dressed like this, in a somber navy pantsuit with a white blouse that covered everything but her face and fingertips—even in this she could make you drool. She hadn't even put the cameo brooch at her throat.

"Mrs. Greener," Everett's tone was flat, "would you tell us, please, why you are seeking custody of your daughter?"

Maricot looked down. When she spoke it was very softly. "Because I feel it is in my child's best interest."

"Will the witness please speak up," said the judge.

"I said, because it's the best thing for my child," Maricot repeated.

Everett addressed her again. "Was there a time you felt differently?"

"Yes. Three years ago. Everything was fine until three years ago."

"What happened then?"

"Thaht was the year Dorothy turned seven," Maricot purred. She can't talk without purring, Dusty was thinking, or walk without being graceful, and why am I thinking these thoughts when I know this bitch is out to castrate me?

"Up to then she'd been Daddy's little girl—oh, they were inseparable at the beginning. But when she got to be seven she started to grow away from him. She wasn't the cute little tomboy anymore. She began to be interested in little girl things. I remember she wahnted to make a dress for one of her dolls, her *poupée,* and she ahsked me to help her. Well, to Dahsty, this was ridiculous. Absurd. A waste of time. What do you want to do *that* for? And other things, like the bahllet—thaht was met with great ridicule, the whole idea of la jeune fille bien élevée. When the Alvin—"

"I didn't quite get that," said the judge.

Everett, who was facing Maricot, turned to the bench. "It's a French expression, Judge. It means well brought up, a well-brought-up young lady. Plaintiff is saying defendant prevented her from bringing up the child in this manner." He faced Maricot again, and she needed no prompting.

"The Alvin Ailey dahncers were giving a dress rehearsal, and I thought it would be beneficial and educational for Dorothy to see it. Well, it so happened that one of Dahsty's comedy clahssics was on that ahfternoon, and he wouldn't let Dorothy out of the house."

It had been Mel Brooks's *The Producers,* but the fight had been about the weather, and dragging the kid out in the cold when she had a stuffy nose.

"It's just been so very difficult to give the child the care and attention she needs when this mahn keeps undermining me at every turn." Maricot, who gestured a lot as she spoke, now clasped her left wrist in her right hand before her, and made an effort to keep still.

Everett was wishing he could do something about that accent, and he was going to have to warn her again about using French. Nevertheless, Everett smiled, obviously pleased with her performance. She was calm and rational, not emotional, not vindictive. And she's the mother, which counts heavily.

"Can you recall any other incidents, Mrs. Greener, in which Mr. Greener undermined, or attempted to undermine, your efforts with Dorothy?"

Mrs. S. was up like a shot. "Leading the witness," she cried.

"I will rephrase," said Everett, before the judge could even rule on the objection. "Mrs. Greener, would you tell us, please, about the telephone call you made to Mr. Greener on the afternoon of August fifth?"

"Yes. I wanted to take Dorothy to Bloomingdale's. He refused to let me. I was going to take her shopping—the child needs clothes. He jahst point-blahnk refused, and used abusive lahnguage into the bargain."

"Specifically, what kind of language?"

"He said, 'Tahff shit.' "

In his seat, Dusty broke up. He couldn't help it. He knew the judge was watching him, but Maricot's dainty elocution was irresistible.

Everett was frowning, as if this were a big deal. "Mrs. Greener, tell us, please, the events that occurred last June the tenth at approximately six in the evening."

"I came home from shopping and found Dorothy in our bedroom, reading one of Dahsty's magazines. An awful magazine. It's called *Hustler*, and it's full of the worst, the most dis*gus*ting—well, let's just say it's not a mahgahzine I want Dorothy to read."

Everett shook his head. He was implying this next question was going to hurt—he hated to put Maricot through this fiery interrogation, but he had to. "Can you tell us explicitly, please, Mrs. Greener, what was the nature of the offensive material?"

Maricot sighed. "Oh, anuses, clitorises, thaht kind of thing, the way the women were posed mostly. Very suggestively, but not in a pretty or attrahctive way at all."

"And what did you do?"

"I took it away from her."

"And what did Mr. Greener do?"

"Well, he became prahctically possessed. He dahshed into the bedroom, snatched the mahgahzine out of my hand, threw it on the bed and began screaming at me. I was making Dorothy uptight about sex, there was to be

"Would you describe the meal you shared there in July of nineteen seventy-four?"

"Yes, sir. We had pizza and soda. Period. And this was not a snack—this was dinner."

Mrs. S. rose again. "Not responsive, Your Honor."

"I will allow it," said Blanchard.

"Who did the ordering?" Everett continued.

"Mr. Greener."

"Were you present at other similar meals?"

"Yes, sir. Once there was takeout food from the Chinese restaurant, and several times Dorothy brought home a Big Mac—you know, a McDonald's burger? And Mr. Greener ate later."

"There is a McDonald's nearby?"

"Right on the corner—yes, sir."

Big deal, and what about the times she's been to Clarke's, and the Brittany, and 21 for Christ's sake?

"Would you say the child was undernourished?"

Mrs. S. was up immediately. She had this springy way of propelling her ass just high enough to get a sentence out before her weight brought her down again. "Leading the witness," she said.

"I will rephrase. How did the child appear to you?"

"I'd say she looked thin. Not, uh, robust."

"What was Dorothy wearing on these occasions?"

"Usually jeans, sneakers, a blouse with a sweater over."

"And what condition were these clothes in?"

"Just okay. There was a hole in one of the sweaters."

"What was your general impression of Mr. Greener's care of the child while Mrs. Greener was away?"

"Slipshod. Careless. Kind of one red sock, one white sock kind of thing."

"And when Mrs. Greener was present?"

"Oh, much better."

"Thank you, Syndee. No further questions."

Syndee made a movement as if to leave the box, but Mrs. S. was suddenly blocking the way down. "Just a moment, Miss Lawrence, please. I'd like to ask you a few things. To start with, do you have any children of your own?"

"No, ma'am."

"When you were growing up, Miss Lawrence, did you ever eat a McDonald's hamburger?"

Everett raised his hand and then thought better of it.

"They didn't have McDonald's when I was growing up."

"Did you ever eat a candy apple at an amusement park?"

"Yes, ma'am."

"Did you ever eat Chinese takeout food?"

"I'm from Toledo, we don't have that."

I'll say you don't, Dusty was thinking, or anything else. I spent two weeks there one Sunday, and all *those* jokes. I got there and it was closed. Second prize, *two* weeks in Toledo.

"Do they have hero sandwiches in Toledo, Syndee? Or what they call subs?"

"Yes, ma'am."

"Did you ever eat one of those?"

"Oh, hundreds." Syndee was smiling her phony Mary Tyler Moore smile.

"Judge, this is immaterial." Everett showed annoyance for the first time. "What the witness ate as a child is not at issue here."

"Trying to establish common custom, Judge," said Mrs. S.

"Move it along," Blanchard said, like a traffic cop. Dusty had never heard a judge speak like that. He suddenly felt the sinking sensation that Dorothy would be swept from him as dust might be swept under a rug—hurriedly, carelessly, impatiently—without thought or concern. *Move it along. Phew.*

"Would you say, Miss Lawrence, that a hero or a sub would be the nutritional equivalent of a McDonald's hamburger?"

"I guess so."

"And having eaten hundreds of those, as a child in Toledo, how do you feel now?"

Syndee looked puzzled. "How do I feel?" She glanced at Everett, but he wasn't looking her way. His chin was on his palm in disgust. "I feel fine."

"How long have you known the Greeners?"

"About five years."

"And over these five years, how many times have you eaten the evening meal there, can you estimate, Miss Lawrence?"

"Oh, I don't know. Dozens."

"How many dozens, Miss Lawrence?"

"I really have no idea."

"Would it be safe to say you've had five hundred meals there?"

"Oh, not that many."

"One hundred meals?"

Syndee was thinking about it. "Maybe seventy-five."

"And of these seventy-five meals, were each of them from McDonald's, Chinese takeout, pizza, or the equivalent?"

"No."

"Can you remember eating any other food at the Greener home?"

"Well, we've had pot roast several times. Mrs. Greener is an excellent cook."

"And Mr. Greener?"

"He can make a good omelette."

"And Dorothy is present at these meals, is that correct?"

"Usually, yes, ma'am."

Blanchard bent forward. "Do you have much more, Mrs. Slotkin?"

"Almost through, Judge," Arline said. "Another five minutes."

Blanchard looked at his watch.

Hey, the sonofabitch just had lunch, what *is* this? thought Dusty. He could see Mrs. S. concentrate on speeding it up.

"Fine, Miss Lawrence, we've established that out of seventy-five meals some were pot roast, some were omlettes, and some were pizza and McDonald's hamburgers. I think you testified to one pizza and soda, one Chinese takeout, and several McDonald's hamburgers."

Blanchard leaned down. "Hold the mustard," he said.

Dusty couldn't believe it. The judge was throwing lines. The entire courtroom was suddenly hysterical; Maricot and Everett were nearly doubled over with laughter, and Raoul was pounding the bench with the flat of his palm, emitting a high-pitched squeak very out of character with his macho image. Blanchard was gazing at them all and grinning smugly. Hey, Dusty thought, *I'll* do the jokes.

Mrs. S. was smiling, and she held it until the room quieted. "How many burgers from McDonald's, Miss Lawrence, have you seen Dorothy eat for her evening meal?"

Syndee thought about it. "Maybe five or six."

"Let's be generous, Miss Lawrence, let's make it eight.

Then, with the pizza and the Chinese takeout, we'll have an even ten meals out of seventy-five. Let's see—are you good at mathematics, Miss Lawrence?"

"I'm good at figures," said Syndee, the first halfway witty thing Dusty had ever heard her say. Blanchard smiled at her, and so did Everett. Christ, Dusty thought, if I had tits I could rule the world.

Mrs. S. was waiting. "All right, then, Miss Lawrence, suppose you tell me how many meals there are in five years. Just counting dinners. And then suppose you tell me what percentage of those meals you'd assume to be pizza, Chinese, or McDonald's."

"Well, five times three sixty-five would be eighteen hundred, and ten out of seventy-five, make it one hundred out of seven fifty, that's two hundred out of fifteen, maybe two fifty out of eighteen—it comes out to about twenty percent."

Hey, thought Dusty—I can book this girl at IBM. She's on the ball where numbers are concerned—so is Maricot. And usually the numbers have an S with two lines through it right up front.

"Miss Lawrence, you're a whiz!" Mrs. S. was congratulating her. "Twenty percent is one out of five. Now, when you were growing up in Toledo, would eating a submarine sandwich every fifth meal have made you thin and—you used a phrase a while back—not robust?"

"I really can't answer that. It might have."

Mrs. S. took a beat's pause. "All right, Miss Lawrence. No further questions."

Blanchard sat up in his chair. "Court is recessed for ten minutes." he said.

It was only five past four but Dusty was tired—he was beginning to sag. Answering Mrs. S.'s questions was tougher than doing comedy. You needed the same energy in delivery, but you had to concentrate harder on your material—there was no set routine, you didn't know where the laughs were, you were floundering, but you hadda come off looking good 'cause this time it's not just a bad report to Leonard—it's the kid.

Ten minutes ago, when Mrs. S. was making him tell about Raoul Mendoza, he'd felt the sickening warning symptoms of an anxiety attack: the sweaty palms and upper lip, the rapid, shallow breathing, the feeling of being very close to the edge of a heart attack. It was at these times that he had to swallow five—sometimes ten—milligrams of Valium. He'd reached into his jacket pocket and extracted one of the little yellow pills. With his dry throat, it had been nearly impossible to work up the saliva needed to get it down.

And this is the *best* it gets. After Mrs. S. was finished, Everett was on deck, waiting for him like a jackal for a weasel. From time to time, as he made his points, he could see the attorney jotting notes on his pad, the bastard. With his gold and onyx cuff links and his smooth graying hair. They gotta call him "The Silver Fox," right? One of *those* guys.

Mrs. S. was getting it all out of him. How Maricot had been screwing Raoul (in *our* bed—very important), how she's away half the time, how she doesn't care about me or the kid or anything but herself. Mrs. S. made him go through the total disintegration of the marriage, and it was a little more than he'd expected. The emotion welling up in his throat met the Valium coming down. Christ, he thought, this is murder. He felt the perspiration under his arms staining his shirt.

Mrs. S. seemed to sense his unhappiness. She held up a pair of fingers. What does *that* mean, for Christ's sake? Two more questions? Two more minutes?

"Now Dusty, I'm going to ask you something unusual, and you may refuse to answer if you wish, but if you do choose to answer, remember you are under oath." Pause. He was learning a lot from Mrs. S. about timing. "I would ask you, Dusty, if you have ever taken drugs."

"No, I have not. I've smoked grass, yes, marijuana, but I've never done hard stuff. I got enough goin' on in my head without drugs."

"Did there come a time in February of nineteen sixty-nine when you were offered a drug called Allocaine?"

"Yes."

"Who made you this offer, and under what circumstances?"

"My wife, Maricot. We were up at the Concord Hotel on a weekend together, and she brought out a jar of this clear liquid and asked me to share it with her."

"And what did you do?"

"Well, I wanted to know what it was, and she said it

was this stuff Allocaine, from the West Indies, that gave you a great high."

"What kind of a high?"

"She said it made you more powerful, you could get into people's minds and control them, you could make people—"

"Just a minute, Dusty." Mrs. S. stopped him. "You mean Mrs. Greener alleged it made you *feel* more powerful?"

"No, no, she said it actually gave you this power. You could control people by entering their minds. She wanted me to smoke this stuff and enter her mind."

"Did you say it was a liquid?"

"It's a tincture. You dip the end of a joint into it, or rub it on with a toothpick. You don't need much—it's very potent."

"In other words, you take it in conjunction with marijuana."

"That's one way. You can put a drop on your tongue. You can bake it into cookies. I don't get into hard stuff. I'll do a joint once in a while."

"So you refused."

"Objection." Everett had been searching for an opening throughout this exchange. Mrs. S. had been careful not to give him one. But he'd found one now. "Leading the witness," he said.

"I will rephrase," Mrs. S. said, quickly, before the momentum died. "How did you respond to Mrs. Greener's offer?"

"I refused."

"And what was her reaction then?"

"She just went ahead and did some herself."

"And was she then able to control your mind?"

Dusty smiled inwardly, remembering the evening. It had been one really memorable screw, he had to admit, all laughing and crying and loving together, passionate declarations and tears of emotion and—the cards! That's right!

"The cards! She was able to guess the cards."

Cards? What cards? Mrs. S. was momentarily off balance. She'd been over this testimony with Dusty three times, and hadn't heard of any cards. She took a breath, and as she spoke she warned Dusty with her eyes to think before he answered.

"What cards are those, Dusty?"

"We had a deck of Tarot cards, and while she was high on Allocaine she told me to turn them up, one by one, and she'd tell me what they were because, see, she was actually making me pick them."

"So the Allocaine actually *gave* her this power?"

"Hey, listen, she got them all right." Dusty hadn't caught her signal. He was coming to Maricot's defense, which was not where Arline wanted to go at all. She steered the questioning back on course.

"To your knowledge, Dusty, is Mrs. Greener a frequent user of this drug?"

"I have seen her take it six times in the past two years."

"All right, Dusty. Now I would ask you to recall a conversation you had with your wife in early November, nineteen seventy-four, dealing with Dorothy's conception."

Everett raised a finger. "Object to this as leading, Judge."

Blanchard cupped his chin in his hand. "Let him answer yes or no."

Dusty saw Everett's lips compress in irritation.

"Yes, I recall the conversation—it was on the telephone. Mrs. Greener was on tour and I called her in Boston."

"And what was the substance of this conversation?"

"How I missed her and wished she were home. A lot of mushy talk, you know how it goes. I said we oughta think about maybe having another child."

"And what was Mrs. Greener's response?"

"She said, 'Forget it. I didn't want the first one.' "

"Did she give a reason for this atttiude?"

"Yes, she said it ruined her figure, that she depended on her figure for dancing."

Everett stood up angrily. "If your honor please, this is not part of this case at all."

Blanchard looked down mildly. "It is part of her attitude toward the child as to whether or not she shall have custody, is it not?"

"I don't think so, Judge."

"No?"

"No."

"That she did not want this child, isn't that material in this consideration?"

Everett was losing his cool for the first time, and Dusty

saw a dangerous gleam in the lawyer's eyes. He paused a moment to regain himself. "Does Your Honor mean whether she wanted to conceive having a child as being material?"

"Insofar as it may affect her present attitude. I will allow it, Mr. Everett." In Blanchard's tone was something of a reprimand. Reverse English. Everett sat down again, glowering, and began tapping his gold-filled pen rapidly into his palm. Blanchard turned to Mrs. S. "Let's go," he said impatiently.

"I'm finished, Judge. I give the witness to Mr. Everett." There was another question Arline had planned to ask Dusty, but she wanted to let Everett cross-examine now, when he seemed irritated. He just might put his well-shod foot in his big mouth.

The lawyer fairly sprang to the witness box, and Arline could see the bone in his jaw moving. She hated doing this to Dusty, but the opportunity wouldn't come again.

Everett, for his part, showed no loss of equilibrium. He spoke to Dusty calmly, in a low tone. But his jawbone was the giveaway.

"Mr. Greener, would you say you were familiar with your daughter's reading habits?"

"Yes, sir." In contrast to his informal manner with Mrs. S., with Everett Dusty was overly polite. He had been warned about his flippancy.

"Then perhaps you can tell me the last book Dorothy read."

"Certainly. It was *In His Own Write* by John Lennon."

"Are you aware she has read *Fear Of Flying?*"

"Yes, sir. I encourage her to read everything she can."

"Including pornography?" He saw Mrs. S. begin her rising bounce and deflected her with an upraised hand. "I will rephrase. Including explicit descriptions of sexual intercourse?"

"Better from books than the kids on the street."

"You're answering yes?"

"Listen, I've got *Playboys*, I've got *Hustlers* all over the apartment. She can read them or ignore them, it's up to her."

Everett suppressed a smile. "And in these magazines, Mr. Greener, isn't it true that you can find the common Anglo-Saxon term for intercourse?"

"Sure. Hey, what are we doing here, Lenny Bruce reruns? She's heard all the words. She goes to Dalton." He caught Mrs. S. giving him a look. The look said, Careful, careful.

Everett studied his pad, took two steps backward. "Mr. Greener, you've stated your wife left your bed and board willfully, and for the purpose of establishing a carnal relationship with Mr. Mendoza."

"Continuing a relationship, yes, sir."

"Oh, really? To your knowledge, how long had she been seeing Mr. Mendoza when she moved out of the apartment?"

"For at least a year."

"And where did these meetings allegedly take place?"

"At my home, on Fifty-fifth Street."

"I see. And where did you get this information?"

"Oh, come on. She admits it."

"Will you answer my question, please? Have you seen Mr. Mendoza in your home?"

"No."

"Have you seen tangible evidence in your home that would indicate a visit by Mr. Mendoza? A hat lying around, for instance, or even his brand of cigarette in the ash tray? Can you state you have tangible evidence to this effect?"

"No."

Everett paused, took his two paces backward. "Mr. Greener, did you ever strike your wife?"

Uh-oh, Dusty groaned inwardly, we're getting into the heavy stuff. "Yes. Once."

"And where was that, please?"

"It was at a party on Central Park West. In the bathroom." No use withholding this—he knew Maricot had spilled it all.

"Did you hit her with your fist?"

"No, I slapped her. Like this." Dusty made a slapping motion with the palm of his hand, swinging out toward Everett. The gesture wasn't lost on the attorney.

"How many times?"

"Once."

"And was the subject under discussion her manner of conduct and dress?"

"Wait a minute. Conduct and dress?"

"How she should dress and what her conduct should be as Dusty Greener's wife."

"I told her not to shake herself around so much when she wore low-cut things. She was being deliberately provocative."

"I see. Do you often have this impulse, to strike your wife?"

Dusty was tempted to say yes, and so will you if you keep seeing her, but what he said was, "No, sir."

"Do you remember threatening to beat Mrs. Greener until—this is a quote—'the excelsior falls out of your head'?"

"Oh, yeah."

"That was in the privacy of your own bedroom, I believe?"

"I believe so."

"And what was the provocation this time? Was she shaking around again?"

This is dumb, Dusty was thinking, really dumb. "I don't remember. There've been so many—" He suddenly caught himself, but it was too late.

"Exactly," the lawyer said softly, underplaying it, but his triumph rang through the courtroom. "There've been so many fights, so many times you've wanted to kill her—*haven't there?*"

"Objection!" Mrs. S. shouted furiously. "Judge, this is a most flagrant leading of the witness!"

Before the judge could rule on this Dusty spoke. "He's right." Arline's eyes went to the ceiling, as Dusty, to his own surprise, gave evidence against himself. "We've had a lotta fights, and often I've been tempted to knock the sh—to let her have it. But I only struck her once. In ten years."

Everett's gaze penetrated a point just above Dusty's nose with laser beam intensity. "Yet you bodily threw her out of the room last June when you found her talking to the child, did you not?"

"Yes, because she was—"

"Yes or no, Mr. Greener?"

"Yes."

Everett paused, letting the word hang like a weight in the air. "And have you not forcibly detained your wife in the bedroom and held conferences with her, preventing her from sleeping until she has cried from exhaustion?"

"I'm the one who was exhausted," said Dusty, but without much conviction.

Everett had succeeded in crushing the spirit out of him. Now the lawyer took those two steps backward that always preceded a change of subject. "Mr. Greener," he began, and his manner was concerned, like a friend. "Are you on any medication?"

"I take Valium." And why the hell isn't it working?

"For what condition?"

"Hypertension."

"I see. And how does this hypertension cause you to behave?"

You're looking at it, buddy, he wanted to say. "I have a tendency to become very emotional under stress. Valium helps control that, and just generally calms me down."

Everett leveled his steely gaze at Dusty. "I would suggest you increase your dosage, Mr. Greener," he said, and took a final pace backward. "No further questions."

Dusty was trembling. He wiped the sweat from his upper lip with the tip of his forefinger. Sonofabitch, that's rough, he thought, and walked shakily down the steps of the witness box.

Somehow they all found themselves trudging out of the courthouse together into the fading autumn twilight. Daylight saving time was nearly over, the city would be back on eastern standard time within a week, and it would feel like fall again. The air was good against Dusty's face, revivifying and cool. He felt as if he'd just gone fifteen rounds with Muhammed Ali. He almost had to lean on Arline's arm for support.

All at once Maricot materialized, on his other side. She was smiling and casual, as if there were no hostility, no mortal combat between them, no trial. She fell into step with him and put her hand on his arm.

"Dahsty, listen," she began. "Are you working Sahturday?"

"Yeah. Why?" Dusty asked her. He was amazed he could exchange two civil words with her after the shit she was putting him through.

"Well, I was thinking maybe Dorothy could have dinner with me anyway, just on Sahturday."

"Sure, Maricot," he said evenly. "As soon as you give back the cha-cha."

She looked at him incredulously. "Dahsty, for heaven's sake, are you going to start with that silly cha-cha again?"

I sure am, he thought. It had been preying on his mind, way at the back, burrowing forward like a mole. I know she has that fuckin' cha-cha. "Send it back anonymously, I don't care, anything. But till we get that cha-cha, no dinners with the kid."

Maricot spun away furiously, rejoined Raoul, and gestured her way angrily and animatedly down the rest of the shallow steps.

Dusty looked at Mrs. S. significantly. She squeezed his arm. "One more day, Dusty, just one more day. And you can go home."

"Would you teach her to be honest and straightforward in her relationships, or devious and deceitful?"

"The ahnswer is obvious."

"Could we hear it, please?"

Maricot shuddered perceptibly. "I would teach her to be honest and straightforward whenever possible."

"Oh, yes? And when not possible, what then?" The words pelted Maricot like grapeshot. "To do what's expedient? To gratify your own selfish pleasures?" Mrs. S. was relentless. "If Dorothy were to marry and then fall out of love with her husband, what would you advise her about relationships with other men?"

Maricot was blinking rapidly. "I'd try and talk her out of it."

"You would? Why?"

Mrs. S. was hammering at Maricot, putting her under tremendous pressure. Now Maricot cracked. She screamed at Mrs. S. "I would do what was necessary! Sometimes there *is* no right thing to do!"

"Can you honestly tell this court you gave even a fleeting thought to Dorothy's welfare when you deserted your husband for Mr. Mendoza?" Arline indicated Raoul with a sweep of her arm.

Maricot regained a measure of composure. "You don't know what goes on in my mind." she said coolly.

"I have some idea," Mrs. S. replied with acidity. "I'm sure it must have occurred to you that breaking up your home would traumatize Dorothy's growth. Yet that didn't stop you, did it, Mrs. Greener?" There was a protracted silence. Arline looked out at the benches, searching for Raoul Mendoza. He was in the middle of the third row, in his T-shirt and leather jacket, his elbow on his thigh, his chin on his fist, glaring at her malevolently. Arline had a flash image of Raoul waiting for her in her vestibule. She swung back to the stand.

"If it came to a choice between Mr. Mendoza and Dorothy, Mrs. Greener, who would you choose?"

"I'd choose Dorothy. I love her more than anyone in the world." Mrs. S. turned away, dismissing Maricot in a faintly contemptuous manner. "That's all, Mrs. Greener," she said, and, as Maricot left the stand, Arline moved directly below Blanchard's dais and began her summation.

"The record shows two parents: one loving, attentive, caring. Responsible. He pays the bills. He takes her to the dentist. He makes sure she has a birthday party. He places her above all others . . . something Mrs. Greener is unwilling to do, though she will not say so. She professes to love her child more than anything in the world. But she will not place her child's welfare above the need for attention from a man who is not her husband." Mrs. S. was speaking slowly now, making sure each phrase was weighted and ringing. "We have heard conclusive evidence of Mrs. Greener's affair—lasting over a year—including, on one occasion, entertaining her paramour in her own marital home while the child was present.

"It is the court's responsibility to act in the best interest of the child. I submit Dorothy Greener's best interest is with the parent who has consistently demonstrated his concern for her and cared for her since the day she was born. That parent is her father, Benjamin Greener."

Arline sat down at her end of the table. Across from her, at the other end, Everett was toying with his gold-filled pen, seemingly lost in his own thoughts. But as soon as the reverberations of Mrs. S.'s speech had died away, he began to speak—still seated in his chair.

"Your Honor, we are asking for a primal right." Everett said. "The return of a child to her natural mother." He placed his pen on the table next to his pad. "We are prepared to admit, we do not dispute, that this mother left her home; she left a malignant and neglectful father from whom she now wishes to protect her rightful child." At this point the lawyer rose, slowly, from his chair and put his butt up against the table's edge, giving himself an air of informality as he crossed his arms over his chest.

"Let's talk about Mr. Greener for a moment. In addition to his work, which, by his own admission, comes in only sporadically, this Mr. Greener is a dangerous man." Pause. "Yes, I said dangerous. I considered the choice of that word very carefully, but what else would you call a man who thinks striking a woman is a matter of little consequence—a man whose ego is so uncontrolled he thinks the rights and considerations of others are meaningless up against his own desires. He is a man without a sense of parental responsibility when measured against the current standards of the community, a man who would willingly expose a ten-year-old girl to flagrantly perverse and shocking depictions of sexual practices. He is a man who will brook no rational argument when balked, who resorts to violence at the least provocation, and who is—indeed—forced to take medication to keep himself under control. I'm sorry, I have to call such a man dangerous." Everett shook his head in sorrow. He had been standing beneath the judge's dais. Now he moved to where Maricot was sitting and nodded his approval.

"By contrast, Mrs. Greener is a loving mother who only wishes to establish a meaningful home for her child. A home where warmth and camaraderie can flourish. Where Dorothy can live far from the unhealthy, pernicious influence of her father." The lawyer swiveled one hundred and eighty degrees to face Judge Blanchard.

"Judge, it is for you to decide which way the twig will bend, whether Dorothy Greener's formative years will be stunted and warped—or whether she will grow up straight and tall, in the sunshine and happiness of a mother's love, to become a shining and useful member of the community."

Everett's voice took a bow, but Blanchard's expression remained impassive. His face revealed nothing. "I will see the child in my chambers," he said, and left the bench in a swirl of black.

7

The cabbie was taking Third Avenue uptown. Cabbies never know anything. Dusty leaned forward and spoke through the perforations in the plastic partition. "If it's all the same to you, let's go across on Fourteenth Street."

"You mean to Eighth?"

"Tenth. Eighth'll be jammed above Forty-second."

"Right. Well, that's why I'm taking Third."

"Yeah, but you'll hit crosstown traffic. Do me a favor, take Tenth." The cab swung west, and Dusty turned to Doe.

"So what'd he ask you?"

"Oh, Frankie, he was really cool. He just said, you know, I'm sure your mom and dad have talked to you and all, but now I want you to tell me without any, you know, um, what they said to you, he said, in other words, don't pay any attention to what you and mommy said before."

"Yeah, so?"

"So I told him wh——"

"What did Mommy say, anyway?"

"Oh, you know." A giggle. "What a creep you were."

"Oh, yeah?"

"Yeah, she really laid you out . . . she said with Raoul we'd be together more and, like, whenever she went on trips we'd always do it together, like a family. I'd be like the other kids, who aren't in The Showbiz." It was one of their jokes—the Feinsteins in the mountains always called it The Showbiz.

"Do you think we're not together enough?"

"No, but she meant, you know—"

"Doe, *please* try not to say 'you know.' "

"All right, but she meant, um, well . . . "

What Maricot had meant was that she was *really* in love with Raoul, *crazy* about him, is what she'd meant, and that she wasn't in love with Dusty anymore. Is what she'd meant. But Dorothy couldn't bring herself to say that to Dusty. It would just kill him.

"So what did Blanchard say?"

Doe was glad Frankie had skipped the hard part. "So he said who do you like to spend time with the best, and it was hard, because I like to do things with you, and I like to do things with Mommy."

"What things with Mommy?" He was interested to hear this.

"I don't know. You know. Oops, sorry. Um, girl things, like trying on clothes. And singing those funny songs."

"The 'chahnts'?"

"Yeah, the chahnts. Like that." There had been a period where Maricot had done Buddhist chanting. She was always trying on some new discipline. Like she split the Saturday after her last est weekend, right?

Anyway, when Doe was seven Maricot went to Buddhist meetings and sat on her feet and chanted till she was blue in the face. And she brought a *gehonzon* home and when Dorothy heard Mommy singing these funny songs she wanted to do it, too. So the two of them would spend whole afternoons doing "The Chahnts." Maricot even threw in a few of her own, in French. Dusty loved that, the idea of Doe learning French. There was one chant in particular.

"Doe, do that *bête* chant for me, wouldja?"

The child closed her eyes, shutting out the traffic and the distraction of bright October sunlight whizzing by. She leaned against him and sang:

Je suis la bête	(I am the beast
Je vis dans ton coeur	I live in your heart
Si tu m'aime bien	If you love me well
Je te donn'rai le bonheur	I'll bring you good luck
Si tu m'aime pas bien	If you don't love me well
La tristesse est ta sort	I'll make you cry
Si tu me rejet	And if you deny me
Je te donn'rai la mort.	I'll make you die.)

Dynamite. What other ten-year-old in history could recite French poetry in one breath and lay a punch line on you in the next? Dusty had this vision of Doe as a woman. She was gonna be the Carole Lombard of the eighties, just the best chick the world had ever seen—she was gonna be sexy and funny and passionate all at once. Doe was a cusp child, November twenty-first, on the line between Scorpio and Sagittarius, a stunning combination with her deep, dark Scorpion eyes that burned right through you (sexy, sexy—in another four, five years, watch out!) and then *pow!* her Sagittarian sense of humor would make you *scream*. Hey, her birthday was coming up soon.

"Whaddaya want for your birthday, honey?" He thought maybe she'd throw some line at him—Promise me anything but give me Arpège, or, A diamond is forever, or something flip, but instead she said, "Could we be together with Mommy?" and it caught him off guard. He bent tenderly over her and kissed the top of her head. "Ask me for something else, will you, sweetheart?"

They stepped out of the dingy elevator and Dusty checked his watch. Two fifteen. Gina wouldn't be home from school yet. "Go remind Mrs. Antonucci we need Gina this weekend," he said to the kid.

"Awww, Frankie, I'm old enough to sit with myself, doncha think?"

"Next year."

"Aww, come on, you always say that."

"Go, schmucko, go."

She crossed the hall petulantly to Mrs. Antonucci's. "Get down tonight," she sang. "Get down tonight." She knew he didn't like her saying dirty things. "Do it anywayou wanna, seven, eight. Do it anywayouwanna, seven, eight."

Christ, just like her mother, counting off the beats. He negotiated the door to his apartment—police lock, top lock, door. You think I'm protected enough?—*I* can't even get in here. He moved through the cramped foyer into the living room and turned on the lamp by the étagère. Two fifteen in the afternoon and the place is pitch black. Christ, we gotta get outta here. There was a window here in the living room, but it looked out on a gray courtyard, and Maricot had long ago hung drapes across the whole wall. Dusty sprawled out on the couch, feeling that nervous kind of tired you get from getting up too early. For court. Thank God that was over. He wished he didn't have to work tonight. He felt like talking to someone, and he picked up the phone and dialed his friend Phil, who was the projectionist for the Bethune Co-op 16mm Cinema. The Beth was a film society two lesbians had organized. They were always screening these dyke-o double bills. A typical program at the Beth would be *Maedchen in Uniform* and *Kansas City Bomber*. For a buck and a half. Dusty's favorite story about Phil the Projectionist was when he loaned the projector overnight to a friend named Jerry, who had some stag films he wanted to run. Phil hated doing it, he was scared to death to let the projector out, but Jerry promised: he said don't worry, I'll have it back by eleven in the morning for your first show. Comes eleven, Phil's in front of the theater, waiting. No sign of Jerry. Eleven thirty. Twelve. No Jerry. Sonofabitch. Phil gets on the phone, there's no answer. Takes a cab to the guy's place, landlady tells him Jerry's father died this morning, he's at the funeral home. Phil's frantic, he runs to the subway, trains out to Woodlawn. There's Jerry in tears, tearing his hair out. The rabbi's saying kaddish. Phil gets behind a tombstone. *Pssst. Pssst,* Jerry! Jerry sees him, waves a wild arm—get away from me! My father's dead! *Pssst.* Jerry, please, the dykes'll beat the *shit* outta me! Get *away* from me, I told ya! But Jerry, you promised. Will you leave me alone! My father's dead!

"Hello?"

"Phil, it's Dusty. How ya doin'?"

"Okay, man. I just got back from my folks'. Tssshhh."

"What're you running this weekend?"

"*The Killing of Sister George* and *The Children's Hour*, the Audrey Hepburn one. You wanna come?"

"Can't. I'm working. Tomorrow, too. Maybe Sunday. Like to see you—how's lunch tomorrow, like one thirty, two o'clock? I'll come down there."

"Okay, man, sure. Entirely possible. Hey, man, can you score me some grass?"

"Yeah, I'll bet I can. One of the band guys can prob'ly deal me a coupla lids."

"I'd really appreciate it. I ran out down at my folks'." Phil's folks owned a liquor store in Frenchtown, New Jersey. "So call me tomorrow, okay?"

"You call me, I'm doing you the favor.'"

"Who wanted to have lunch?"

"Fuck you, whose dime is this?"

"Hey, man, you know it's hard for me, I'm in the booth."

Dusty grinned. "All right, but it's gonna cost you." He hung up as Doe entered the living room and went straight to the radio on the étagère, which was a Marantz receiver. I'm lucky to have that receiver, Dusty reflected. I'm lucky the bitch left me toilet paper.

"—real live no jive ninety-nine XLO T-Shirt to the first three callers who reach me, the real Jack Steele, at eight six six, nine two hundred, that's—"

"Doe, do me a favor and play RVR for just ten minutes, wouldja? I'm not up to— Owwww!" Dusty suddenly clutched his temples.

"Frankie, what is it?"

"Owwww! Aaaahhhh, Christ!" It was pain, pain so intense he thought he might pass out. The pain ran between his temples, as if a laser gun had fired a beam of agony into his ear—he could visualize the searing orange line running through his skull. "Owwww!" he cried again, and fell to the floor, rubbing his temples with the heels of his hands. Doe was terrified. Was it his ears? She turned the radio off.

"Frankie, what is it—what *is* it?"

"I don't know! Owwww! Oh, Jesus, Doe, call the hospital, call the ambulance, get me some help. . . . Aaaahhh! Christ!" Doe ran to the phone, tears spilling down her face.

"Wait, wait, wait a minute . . . wait . . . it's going away . . . ohh, oh, my God, dear Jesus, sweet Jesus. . . ." Dusty lay in a crumpled heap on the floor, his chest and belly expanding and contracting with deep inhalations.

"Oh, Holy God, Doe, I hope nothing like that, I hope you never have to go through anything, ahn . . . like that . . . Jesus. . . . "

"What happened, Frankie? What?" There was fear in her eyes. She was very disturbed. He was catching his breath. "It was this incredible cutting pain . . . right in the center of my head . . . I don't know where it came from. . . ."

He stopped.

Doe was staring at the wall in amazement. "Frankie . . . look."

Dusty followed her gaze to the wall. Where the assator had hung its shape was outlined now by a slightly whiter area—like the patch behind a picture when you take it down. Doe was gazing at this area in wonder. Suddenly she blanched. Dusty saw her hand go to her mouth in horror..

"What is it, Doe?"

"Frankie, I'm scared," she said, and moved closer to him, for she had seen the patch on the wall puff out like a balloon, turn from white to red, and then pulsate, changing from bright crimson to dark scarlet—like oxygenated and deoxygenated blood.

8

The memory of his attack still haunted Dusty when he met Phil for lunch at the Trattoria Da Alfredo Saturday afternoon. They split an order of Carbonara and he told Phil the whole saga of Maricot's desertion and the suit for custody. Phil sucked up the spaghetti like a vacuum cleaner. When he spoke little droplets of cream sauce splattered across the table.

"But, man, I don't understand. She's the one who split. What's her problem?"

"What's her problem? She wants the kid."

"Just to give you grief, man? That's the pits."

Dusty laughed. "That's just a fringe benefit. She wants to run the kid's life, she wants to play God."

"You oughta meet my new chick, man," said Phil. "She doesn't think kids should even be born, much less raised." He paused reflectively. " 'Course she is a dyke," he added.

Dusty stared at him. "You're going with a dyke, Phil?"

Phil smiled a smile full of cream. "Man, you gotta try it, it's the greatest. No responsibilities, no commitments, she never lays any of that let's-get-married shit on me. She brings home the bread. All I have to do is cook and wash the dishes."

Dusty grinned. This is why you had to see Phil at least once a month. "Yeah, but Phil, what's it like in the sack?"

"Man, I'm learning things I never even *thought* of. She talks to me through the whole thing—do this, do that, not so hard, not so fast—"

"That would drive me nuts, a chick directing me like at."

"You gotta think of it as a learning experience, man. Listen, didja get me some grass?" Dusty dug in his shirt pocket and produced one fat, professional-looking joint. Phil's face fell.

"All I could get, Phil. Cat says if you want he can get you some next week?"

"For how much?"

"Forty. He says it's dynamite stuff."

"You trust him?"

Dusty nodded.

"All right, I'll do this joint and let you know." He rolled the joint appraisingly between his fingers. "So you gonna get the kid?"

"Yeah, I think so. This lady lawyer said she was like eighty percent sure."

"Must be fun having a kid. Does she dig Audrey Hepburn? Why don't you bring her to the show tomorrow? You working tonight?"

"Yeah. I'll call you when I get up." Dusty finished the last of his Macon Blanc and threw a five-dollar bill on the table. "Gotta go to Pennsylvania," he said, and ran across Eighth Avenue to catch the Number 10 bus uptown.

He picked up his tux at the house and stood by what he called the snailevator, impatiently pressing the bell. When the door opened, Dodo popped out. "Hi, sweetheart, gotta run."

"Frankie, wait a minute. Gina asked me to make sure we had the good ice cream in the freezer—you know, the Häagen-Dazs. We're out of it."

Dusty dug in his pocket. "All right, here, go to the fat man's." He gave her two singles and stepped inside the elevator. "And go easy on it, I don't want you looking like P——" He dropped his voice. "—looking like Piggy Gina."

Dodo squealed delightedly and ran into the house.

The Lincoln Tunnel loomed up like a bright mouth as Dusty wearily paid his dollar fifty and was routed by a line of orange witches hats into the left lane. Almost home. God, what a haul to make in one night.

He'd left the Host Farms, where the food was good and his room was comfortable, two hours and twenty minutes ago because he wanted to be home with the kid. Maybe the trial would turn out to be a blessing in disguise. Maybe he'd value time with Dorothy more now.

He wondered if the girls had finished off the ice cream. He was sure Gina had, the little glutton. Christ, there's a porkosity if I've ever seen one, he thought—always putting something in her mouth. And hair on her upper lip. She was outta the room when the sex appeal was passed around, that's for sure. God, a roll of the dice. He just knew everything was gonna work out right for Doe—she was gonna grow into such a sweet bundle. There was nothing you wouldn't do with Doe—her feet, her armpits, her box, her little ass—they were gonna be even sweeter than her mother's. But let one guy start coming on to her —he suddenly found himself resenting Doe's future lovers. Look at me, he thought, a textbook case. The jealous Dad.

Police lock, top lock, door. Hey, hold on. The police lock opened to the left, but his key met no resistance. None on the top lock, either. Only the bottom lock sprung against the key with any pressure. He pushed the door open and walked past the kitchen into the living room. What he saw was right out of a 1945 Dick Powell private-eye picture.

Well, not quite. In a Dick Powell picture, the furniture would be all over the place—tables overturned, lamps broken. Not here. Everything was in order, relatively undisturbed, except for Maricot's dressing table chair, which had been moved from the bedroom to the living room. Sitting on this chair, her wrists and ankles bound with two-inch adhesive tape, was Gina. Four more strips of tape secured Gina to the chair, two across her thighs, two across her breasts. She was nearly mummified.

Her eyes met Dusty's and in that moment he knew Dorothy was gone. He took the adhesive on Gina's mouth, and with one quick stroke tore it away. Gina barked in pain.

"Where's Dorothy?"

"Oh, Mr. Greener, they took her, they took her away." Gina was terrified Dusty was going to be mad at her.

"Who took her?" he asked, though he already knew. He was unwinding the tape from her wrists. It made a sound like paper tearing.

"Mrs. Greener and that man, you know—"

"Yeah, I know. What time was this?"

"It was just after twelve, because we were getting ready to watch the 'Midnight Special'—"

"How'd they get in?"

"Well, it was Mrs. Greener, and I thought, you know, it would be okay." He could have killed her then, without any compunction at all, taken her pudgy neck and wrung it between his fingers.

"Did they say anything—think, Gina—*any*thing about where they were going?"

"The airport."

"Did they mention what airline, what time the flight was?"

"No, Mr. Greener . . . " she blurted out, and as he unwrapped her ankles Gina began to cry. Little, choked-back, dry sobs of relief, exhaustion, and fear of being held accountable. At four fifteen in the morning.

Dusty kneeled by the chair and held her, rocking her back and forth in his arms. He smelled the unpleasant odor of bad breath and sweat and for thirty seconds or so had to breathe through his mouth.

"All right, Gina, it's okay, they're gone. I'm not mad at you, honey, I know it wasn't your fault." They should gimme an Academy Award for *this* performance, he thought. "Just tell me what happened, from the 'Midnight Special' on. Don't leave anything out."

"Can I get a glass of juice?" Gina asked, and he knew she was okay now—her mind was back on food. "Yeah, sure, here—you want me to get it for you?"

"That's all right." She crossed into the kitchen, opened the fridge, and stood there uncertainly, her eyes taking in the shelves.

She came back into the living room bearing a glass peanut butter jar full of grapefruit juice. She sat on the couch and took a big gulp. "We were watching the 'Midnight Special.' Helen Reddy was on," she began, and Dusty thought, Spare me the lineup, please, but he didn't interrupt.

"—and somebody knocked on the door."

"How'd they get in downstairs?"

"I don't know, Mr. Greener, maybe somebody else buzzed them in."

Or maybe they jimmied the door, Dusty thought, and then he remembered Maricot still had her keys. It would've been dumb to alert the girls. Catch 'em off guard, much better.

"So there was this knock on the door, and I went to see who it was, and she said, 'It's Mrs. Greener, Gina, I have something for Dorothy,' and I didn't even think, I just opened the door—"

"Did you have to undo the chain?"

"No, we leave the chain off in case, you know, in case we have to go across the hall for something." Right. Sure.

"So you opened the door and what happened?"

"So I opened the door and Mrs. Greener pushed me, she gave me a big push, and then they both came in and Mrs. Greener told Dorothy to put her coat on 'cause they were gonna take a trip. And all the while she was speaking, that man—you know, what's his name, he comes around here sometimes?"

"Mendoza."

"That's right, Mr. Mendoza—he's unwrapping this adhesive tape and cutting it with a scissors. Look, here's the scissors." She waddled off the couch to the étagère, and picked up a pair of stationery store scissors, holding them for Dusty to see, as if this demonstration would prove what she said was true.

Dusty sighed. Obviously a lot of preparation had gone into this. "And then what?"

"And then Mr. Mendoza said he was sorry, but he was gonna have to tie me to the chair with the adhesive tape. . . . " Dusty could see the tears about to start again. Gina's lower lip was trembling. "He said it in this real nice voice, and he said he was sorry, but he . . . he made me sit in the chair . . . and . . . "

"All right, Gina, it's over now, and you're okay, aren't you?" Gina nodded mutely. "Okay, so now while Mr. Mendoza's doing all this, what was Dorothy doing?"

"She . . . she asked Mrs. Greener if you, you know, if you knew about this, and Mrs. Greener said no, you didn't, and then Dodo said maybe we should wait till you hours? You want her to tell you baby-sitters get extra to be tied up?" She was barking at Dusty accusingly.

"Mrs. Antonucci, you have every right to be outraged," said Slander, "but don't yell at Mr. Greener. He's not the one who put your daughter through four hours of bondage. You can press charges against Mendoza and have him locked up."

"For a year maybe? So that when he gets out he can come carve Gina up with a knife? *Grazie, grazie tanto."*

"Mrs. Antonucci," Dusty interjected, "please, the only way I can get the police to start looking for Dorothy is if you'll press charges against Mendoza. Gina, don't you want to see him punished for what he did to you?" Gina looked uncertainly at her mother and Dusty knew then the ball game was over.

"Just let him stay away, that's all I want. And if you get that little *stronza* back, you keep her away from Gina, you understand?"

Mrs. Antonucci continued to rail against Dusty as he crossed the hall back to his apartment. Go fuck yourself, he thought. Your kid has hair on her lip. She couldn't get laid if she came out of a cake at a prisoners' convention.

Inside he flopped down in the bedroom, reached under the night table, and pulled out the Manhattan telephone directory. Okay, he thought, I'm back at square one. He flipped the book open to Eldridge, Estaban, Evans—ah, there he is: Everett, Lytell, atty 405 Park Ave. Yeah, well not on Sunday. Wait, Res 19 Meridien Lane, Fairfield, Conn. Let's try it, and he dialed 203 and the number, and a woman picked up the phone.

"Hello?"

"Hello, this is Mr. Greener, may I speak to Mr. Everett, please?"

"Yes, hold on. Lye, it's for you." Her voice rang through what sounded like a large, uncarpeted area—maybe the patio, the phone by the pool. Dusty pictured Everett in the sun, at a table beneath an umbrella, in a Lacoste shirt and shorts, lunching on crabmeat in half an avocado, a pitcher of Bloody Marys within reach.

"Yes?" Everett's tone was polite but businesslike.

"This is Dusty Greener, Mister Everett. I have a change of address for Maricot. What did she leave you, Chicago?"

There was a pause. Then Everett said, "I don't know what you're talking about."

"Maricot told me she left you an address where to contact her, but it's been changed. She left you Chicago, right?"

"Mr. Greener, where your wife is is of no concern to me. You will receive the decision in your case in the next week or so. Meanwhile, please have the courtesy not to bother me at my home." And click. Dusty was left with a dead receiver. As he placed it in its cradle he pondered Everett's response. For some reason he believed the attorney. Maricot hadn't told him where she was going. With an effort he pushed himself to his feet, feeling groggy from the Valium and too little sleep. His eyes felt as if he'd just come out of a chlorinated swimming pool, there were rings of color around everything, and the sound of Sunday traffic on the street seemed abnormally loud.

He slipped on his leather jacket, went out to Ninth Avenue, and waited twenty minutes before the number 11 bus arrived to take him down to Twenty-third Street and Raoul's apartment.

He got there about three twenty. Two blocks further west, over by the pier, a big Norwegian freighter sat in the river. If I got on that ship, Dusty wondered, would it take me to Dodo? The building had a three-step stoop, chipped away over the years, and much graffiti, in black spray paint, decorated the pocked stone. "Avengers," Dusty read, and, inside a heart, "Stanley Delphond 1975." The entrance hall floor was tiled—octagonal, bathroom-size tiles—and the mailboxes were rusty with years of oxidization. Dusty skimmed them, searching for the name Mendoza. There *was* no Mendoza, but apartment 3D showed an empty strip where the nameplate had been, and the strip was clean enough to make Dusty think the name had been removed recently—like the night before. In 3C lived someone named Gonzales. Dusty pressed this bell. Without waiting, he tried the front door. The door rattled loosely in its frame, but the latch held firm. Shit, Dusty thought, if I had a credit card I could do it easy.

He was not being buzzed in. He pressed 3A and 3B. When they didn't answer he pressed all the bells, indiscriminately. It was like a house of the dead, or else everyone was on vacation. Well, he thought, I'll just sit here turned it over. *Strength and Health.* On the cover were Mr. and Mrs. Muscle, on the beach showing off their pectorals. Right, gotta keep in shape. Dusty tossed the magazine away and went into the bathroom. In the empty tub (which, unlike Dusty's, was spotless) sat a big wooden cannon cradle, the kind that tips, the kind that holds brandy bottles. In the cradle was a mammoth tinted bottle, the kind that sits atop a water cooler. Dusty read the lettering in the green glass: Saratoga Geyser Water, Saratoga Springs, New York. So that's how he does it, safflower oil and distilled water, hey, hey. Dodo would take that bottle home and put a giant fern or something in it. He had the impulse to bring it home and keep it for her. He pushed this out of his mind and walked back into the room, wandering aimlessly, not knowing what to look for, just hoping something, somehow, would give him some kind of lead. . . .

"Gonzales, tell me, do you know where Mister Mendoza went?"

The Cuban gave his little shrug. "No, I no know. Jus' go away."

Dusty swung his head despondently from side to side. "Gee, that's tough. I got all this money for him." He glanced at Gonzales. "I'm sure it'd be worth something to Mister Mendoza if I could locate him. Maybe as much as fifty dollars." He saw the man furrow his brow.

"Say, you coo' talk to Mees Haideeson. Chee use' to be frens wi' heem."

"Miss—?"

"Haideeson. She een t'ree A."

"Let's go." Dusty held the door as Gonzales shuffled out. There was a piece of paper or something stuck to Gonzales's heel. The Cuban struck if off his shoe with a quick stroke of his hand, and as it hit the floor Dusty saw a color illustration, done in green. Stooping to retrieve it, he saw the drawing was of the bottom half of a green horse, and the texture of the paper was like light cardboard—probably the cover of a softback book. There was the fragment of a phrase in the lower left corner "eeing Tours." He turned it over and saw more printing: "obil Travel Guide

ings Virginia

ite Sulphur Springs, West Virginia

Sonofabitch, it was a *Mobil Travel Guide!* Dynamite,

fuckin' dynamite! This was a clue! He had a lead! His teeth gritted together in anticipation, and at the same moment he saw Gonzales waiting for him down the hall at 3A. He let the apartment door close behind him, but not all the way. He might want to return. He joined Gonzales as he knocked on the door.

"Mees Haideeson . . . Mees Haideeson."

There was a momentary pause and then a woman's voice said, "Who is it?"

"Ees meester Gonzales. I have a fren' here, has some money for Raoul."

The handle turned, and there in the doorway stood not a bad-looking woman. She was about thirty, Dusty judged, with dark, close-cropped hair and a nice figure, which was clothed now in white slacks and a long-sleeved black T-shirt that said Rolls-Royce across her chest. Behind her Dusty could hear a football game on television.

She looked quickly from Gonzales to Dusty, appraising him instantly and so professionally that Dusty knew she was in the people business. Probably a hooker. She was about to say what do you want when Dusty spoke.

"Hi, my name is Greener. I'm looking for Raoul Mendoza, and Mr. Gonzales here said you might be able to help me." He spoke carefully, softly, in a voice designed to induce cooperation.

"Well, Mr. Gonzales is wrong," said the woman. "I have no idea where he is."

She knows something, Dusty thought. Talk to her, talk to her. "You watching the Jets?" Dusty inquired. "What's the score?"

"They're behind, twenty-one to seven, end of the third quarter. You a Jets fan?"

"I've got money on this game," Dusty lied. He saw her thinking it over.

"I'd like you to give me a fast five minutes—though I'll tell you, I usually only talk to people who drive Bentleys." That did it. Her mouth didn't smile, but her eyes gave him points. She stepped back, giving him room to pass.

"Mr. Gonzales," Dusty called over his shoulder, "if I speak to Mr. Mendoza I'll let you know."

"Don' forget," said Gonzales as the door shut in his face.

The room was small, but comfortable. Dusty decided to sit on the convertible couch, but first he crossed to the TV set. "May I?" he asked. She nodded and he turned the volume off. The picture flashed tiny shadows into the room.

She was lighting a Kent, squinting at him over the flame. "You a friend of Raoul's?"

"Not exactly. I told Mr. Gonzales I had some money for him, but that's not true." He looked at her. "Are you a friend of Raoul's?"

"Mm-mm. No, unh-unh. Raoul and I stopped being friends some time ago."

"I'm glad to hear that. Now I can stop playing this stupid game. Listen, ah—by the way, my name is Dusty. What'll I call you?"

"Terri's fine. I don't know what I can tell you about Raoul. He left last night, with that black bitch. That's about all I know."

"Did they say, did they give any indication—"

"No, they didn't, but if I know Raoul, they're going someplace warm."

"Why do you say that?"

"Raoul hates the cold. He spent fourteen years of his life in Nova Scotia, you know."

"No, I didn't know. I thought he was from Puerto Rico or somewhere."

"He is, but he caught fish in Nova Scotia when he was a kid, and he hated it. He used to tell all kinds of stories about getting up at five in the morning to make the goddamn grunion run or salmon or whatever the hell it was." She must have caught him looking at her in a way that said, I want to ask another question but I'm not sure how you'll take it. So she said, "Oh, yes, Raoul and I had a thing for a while. In fact I even moved here because of him. But it ended, and frankly, it was too much trouble to relocate. It didn't matter that much, you know?" She stubbed out her cigarette. "So what do you want him for? Does he owe you money?"

"Worse than that. He ran off with my kid."

Terri Edison gave him a surprised look. "That doesn't sound like Raoul. Raoul isn't interested in anybody he can't punch out or fuck."

"The kid was part of a package. Along with the black bitch." He realized he could finally stop defending

Maricot to people who thought of her as a black bitch. "All right, Terri, I'm gonna list seven towns for you. Tell me if you associate any of them with Raoul, okay?"

"Okay."

Dusty read the towns off from memory, starting with Miami, hitting Kansas City and Chicago, Boston and Washington, and ending with Atlanta and New Orleans.

"You can forget Kansas City and Chicago," Terri said. "Too cold this time of year. I never heard him mention Washington, but I think he did some dealing in Boston. Big college town, you know. Lots of kids." She toyed with her cigarette lighter. "He likes Boston."

Dusty considered it. Maricot liked Boston too. She'd done the ever-popular *Sweet Charity* at that dinner theater up there. Still, it didn't feel like far enough away. If you're splitting New York you don't go to Boston.

"As for Miami, Raoul wouldn't get it on there at all. Unless maybe it was a jumping-off point for Puerto Rico."

"I'm sticking to the States," Dusty said, thinking how hopeless it would be to check international flights.

"Your best bet is the South, if you're asking me. Atlanta, New Orleans, and, yeah, maybe Miami. Maybe. Raoul has a thing for water. As long as it's warm water." Terri rose and walked out of the room. Dusty heard her open an icebox door. He stood up and examined the bookshelves, something he always got a kick out of doing. Kierkegaard, Nietzsche, Kant, Hegel, and Spinoza. She was a hooker all right.

Terri came back into the room with a glass filled with ice in each hand and a can of Diet Pepsi under her arm. Dusty took the can from her and his knuckles brushed her biceps.

"You're a working girl, aren't you, Terri?" he said to her.

She cocked an eyebrow at him. "What makes you figure that?"

"I dunno. Your philosophy books."

"Oh, is that the mark of a working girl?"

"No, but you're the kind of chick—most guys won't see past your boobs—but you got more to offer than that, so after a few years of being treated like a body you figure, Okay, let 'em pay for it."

was sitting on the floor, reading a copy of *Chic*. "Pulling your putz again?" Dusty said, and Phil looked up.

"Hey, man, where were you? I called you this afternoon, see if you wanted to bring Dorothy down. No answer."

"Dorothy's gone. They kidnapped her."

"No shit, man, really?"

"Yeah. They've split. I got a lead on where they might be, though. It's either Kansas City or New Orleans. I'm goin' home and call the hotels, see if I can trace 'em."

"You know what you do, man? Call collect and ask for them by name. Hey, I got this friend Hauser, works for the phone company—he's hipped me to all the phone scams, man. You wouldn't be*lieve* the ripoffs this guy is into. Last Wednesday we called Norway, I mean *Nor*way, man. Just for kicks. These chicks're talkin' to us like 'Euy weeyull koe-nect ewe.' We asked 'em what the weather was like and everything."

"Where's this?"

"Up at Clairol, on Park. These big companies, conglomerates, man, they keep tie lines open to LA, to Europe, to Mexico. We sign in at night, dig? We just flash Hauser's phone company ID and sign some off-the-wall name. And we go upstairs and use the phones. Hey, you want me to fix your bell so you don't get waked up? I can do it, Hauser showed me, you open your phone up and inside there's these bells, man, and between 'em there's a clapper, dig? You just tape some cotton to one of the bells, man, immobilize the clapper when it's on soft. You can do it with a fuckin' band-aid. You gotta meet Hauser, man, he's the end. He's got more scams working."

"Listen, Phil, lend me ten bucks, will you?"

"Aw, shit, man. You hadda spoil a great evening."

"All right, never mind, I'll cash a check with Cheryl." He pulled the door open.

"Hey, that Cheryl digs you, man," Phil said. "You know that? Why don't you get it on with Cheryl sometime?"

" 'Cause I don't like sucking cock," Dusty said, and left.

~ 10 ~

He stopped at the Fat Man's on Fifty-fourth and Eighth, the little deli they always went to, and picked up a couple of knackwurst. He brought the food to the counter by the door. The Fat Man wore heavy, Coke bottle lenses and he wheezed when he spoke.

"How's my little angel today? Or should I say my little devil?"

"She's fine, thanks." Dusty didn't feel like letting the entire neighborhood in on his life, although by this time he was sure Mrs. Antonucci had broadcast it to the whole building. The Fat Man plucked a roll of cherry Lifesavers from the candy display by the register. "For my little angel," he said, and Dusty nodded his thanks and went upstairs.

While the water was boiling, he called the first four motels in New Orleans; The Capri, the Days Inn, the De La Poste (three stars) and the Gateway (formerly the Ramada Inn). No Greener, no Mendoza, and no one who checked in last night or early this morning who answered to the description of a) a little girl, b) a beautiful Haitian woman, c) a well-built guy with curly hair.

He opened a bottle of Sylvaner, poured himself a glass

as the specials cooked, and between sips he called the Hilton Inn, the five Holiday Inns, and the two Howard Johnsons.

He scooped a forkful of mustard onto his plate and dialed the International American Motor Inn, La Quinta, and Le Richelieu. Then there were the two Travelodges, the Patio, the Provincial, two Quality Inns, one Ramada Inn, three Rodeways, two Sheratons, the Sentry, the Siesta, the Vieux Carré Motor Lodge, and a partridge in a pear tree.

Thirty-one motels, and not a lead. He leaned wearily back on the living room couch, realizing only now how fatigued he was. This was his pattern. He ran in spurts, pushing and pushing himself, his mind and body so engaged and into it that he rarely experienced fatigue until —like now—it suddenly caught up with him. He was lucky he'd quit smoking, otherwise he knew he'd be a prime candidate for heart attack. He was nuts enough about his ticker anyway, with the goddamn hypertension.

Syndee Lawrence.

Unless this had been a completely last-minute decision, Maricot had to have told somebody where she was going. Syndee Lawrence was the logical choice. He got up off the couch. Long ago he had put Syndee's number in his book, as a person who always knew where Maricot was. Dusty kept two books, one filled with frequently called numbers, and another—book two—with the names of people on his mailing list, people who got flyers whenever he appeared anywhere. This book was in the little hall opposite the kitchen, in the two-drawer file cabinet with his pictures, his comedy material, and his family papers, like Dorothy's birth certificate and his life insurance (If you call this living). He remembered with a pang of anxiety that this month's premium bill was stuck in the Chock Full O'Nuts can (the urgent-bill can) in the kitchen. That was one bill he'd been on time with, ever since Doe was born. He'd let the car go, the gas, even the rent, but that insurance got paid up. He would have to call AGVA and have that policy rewritten, now that Maricot was no longer part of the family, he thought, as he brought Book Two into the living room and sat down on the couch. A long day. He knew if he lay down in the bedroom he'd fall asleep, and he had to check these hotels before the trail grew cold. And there was still Kansas City.

Syndee lived on West Seventy-fourth Street. Dusty dialed and a guy answered with a big, forceful "Yello."

"Like to speak to Syndee, please."

"She can't come to the phone now. Who's this?"

She was probably in the john. "Tell her Dick Miller wants to talk to her." Dick Miller was an agent who often booked dancers. He knew this would get her to the phone. Sure enough, ten seconds later there she was.

"Hi, Dick." The voice was cheery-bird, squeaky-clean, corn-fed, Midwest sexy. God, how these chicks could act.

"Syndee, this is Dusty Greener." He could feel the shock on the other end of the line. "Now listen—Maricot and Raoul kidnapped Dorothy." He listened again, carefully, for some reaction, some giveaway he could use. There was none.

"I've notified the police, but I really don't wanna get involved with that." The hell he didn't. "Now I want you to give me Maricot's number, where she is, so I can talk to her before I have to send the cops after her." He paused to let this sink in.

"I don't care what she told you, she probably told you not to tell me, didn't she?" He was conscious of a dull ache in his belly. I ate too fast, he thought. Like always.

"But if you want to make it easier on Maricot, Syndee, you'll tell me where I can reach her. Now where is she?"

"I don't know, Dusty, and that's the truth." The Golden Goddess was gone from her voice now; she was a little girl on a tightrope. "She called just before she left. She said she wasn't sure where she was going, but she'd let me know when she got there."

Aha! Dusty's mouth set in a grim smile. Now we're getting somewhere. His stomach began actively hurting. What the hell was it, gas?

"I tell you what, Dusty. When Maricot calls me I'll ask her if she wants you to have the number. I'll tell her what you said, about the police and all, and she can make her own decision."

"Listen, Syndee, will you ask her to call me?"

"I'll do what I just told you I would, Dusty. That's the best I can do. Good-bye." And *click.* A searing, knifelike pain was tearing at his lower abdomen. He was forced down to a kneeling position on the floor, clutching his belly.

"Aaaaannnhh . . ." he moaned, involuntarily, as the

pain grew so intense he thought he'd pass out . . . . Christ, it was the same as his head the other day. Aaaanhhh, Chriiiiisssst. And then he felt himself voiding his dinner, he was messing his pants. Ach, with that terrible wet sickly feces smell and that feeling when you can't control your bowels. Oh, my God, the pain and the shitting and a horrible shortness of breath all at once. God, how am I standing this, it's too much, too much pain, aaaaannnhhh, Chrisssst. And he wrenched and writhed his helpless body about on the carpet and vaguely thought, somebody's sticking pins in my doll, and dimly he heard the big ash tray fall to the floor as his body pulled the area rug away under the coffee table, and it was so wet and horrid in the crack between his buttocks, and, Christ, he couldn't help himself there was no way to stop it, and without knowing it (all he knew was the pain) he began to cry from the pain and the agony of humiliation and helplessness and then a final stab of pain, Too much, too much, and finally he passed into blackness.

When he came to it was six fifteen in the morning, and the first thing he became conscious of was his own stench, filling the room. Christ, it was horrible, like an army latrine. At least the pain had stopped. Jesus, first my head and now this. Maybe I should see Dr. Zahm. Just what I need now, to come down with creeping crud or something.

He got up from the floor, stiff and cramped, and moving very carefully, loosening his belt as he headed into the bathroom. He turned on the shower. Yuucchhh, I'll have to burn these clothes, like a plague victim, he thought.

He came out of the shower feeling disoriented. The sun was shining into the bedroom at an unfamiliar angle. He was usually asleep at this hour. He lay down on the bed, picked up the phone, and opened the *Mobil Guide* to Kansas City. Dully, he started with the Capri Motel (color TV, heated pool, pets limited) and went through thirty-five more in the KC area without turning up anything.

At nine thirty he called Phil, woke him up. "Phil, listen, sorry to wake you, but I need your friend's number—the one who works for the phone company.." He waited while Phil got it together.

"Uh . . . yeah. His name's Frank Hauser . . . call eight one one. He usually gets in around ten." There was a barrage of noise as Phil tried to replace the receiver.

He waited till ten fifteen and then called the New York Telephone Company business office.

"Two one seven. Frank Hauser." (Snuff.) The guy obviously had some kind of sinus condition. He snorted into the phone like an elephant. "Frank, my name's Dusty Greener. I'm a friend of Phil Bournes."

"Oh, yes." (Snuff.) "How is Phil?"

"He's fine. He said you'd be able to help me. I have kind of a deal for you. Could we possibly have lunch today?"

"No, today's bad. I gotta go downtown." (Snuff.) "Pick up some equipment."

"I'll do that with you. I don't mind. Where do you have to go?"

"Cortlandt Street." (Snuff.)

"Fine. I'll meet you. What time? Where are you anyway?"

"I'm at the business office on Thirty-first and Seventh." (Snuff.) "All right, you meet me here at twelve thirty, okay? In the lobby." (Snuff.)

"What do you look like?"

"I'm, uh, kind of heavyset." (Snuff.) "Kind of, uh . . . " (Snuff.)

"I'll find you. Twelve thirty. Thirty-first and Seventh."

"Right." (Snuff.) "G'bye."

Dusty hung up, cutting off the last snort. He wondered if a guy like that got laid much. Must be rough, he thought as he dressed, snorting on top of someone while you were balling. Maybe it produced some crazy rhythms.

He went out to get some cash. His bank was the Chase Manhattan at Fifty-seventh and Broadway. He stood in line behind the rope as the lunch-hour crowd began to trickle, then pour, into the bank. It was eleven forty-five.

"And could you check my balance, please?" He had just taken out a hundred and twenty dollars cash. He figured he'd have to lay at least fifty on Frank Hauser, and he needed some cassette tapes and food and general living shit and . . . Oh God, I hope Doe is okay—what if she tries to get away and they get rough with her? I'll kill that bitch and her stud too if they touch one hair on her head. . . . Do you suppose maybe Doe can sneak out a letter, a postcard? Prob'ly not, they're prob'ly watching everything she does, those bastards. Those bastards!

The girl came back with a white slip on which she had

written his balance after the withdrawal and he shuddered as he walked over to Seventh Avenue. Eighteen dollars and eighty-five cents. Minus the ten he'd cashed with Cheryl last night, made it eight eighty-five. How do I live like this? he wondered. On the edge of oblivion, kiting checks over the weekend, borrowing on Thursday to pay back on Monday. He hoped Leonard had some work for him this weekend.

Frank Hauser was more than heavyset—he was fat. But it wasn't a weight problem, it was a height problem. If he were about eleven foot six he'd be perfect. Hauser stood in the lobby in a rumpled tweed jacket he could not possibly button, his tie circled his throat in a tight ring. Dusty knew him on sight. Hauser was the fat kid everybody ribbed, the kid who made firecrackers in his basement out of a box of Crayolas and some Kolynos toothpaste.

"Frank? I'm Dusty Greener."

"Gladda meetcha." (Snuff.) And the handshake that ate Chicago. The snorting happened every ten or twelve seconds, regardless of whether or not he was speaking. "Let's go," said Hauser with a snort, "subway's this way."

"I'll spring for a cab, Frank, okay? Hard to talk in the subway." Hauser shrugged and swung his bulky form out onto Seventh Avenue. This was one fat guy who made a liar out of a cliché—he had no odd grace at all. Dusty nearly had to push his fat ass into the taxi. Luckily they were below the garment-center crush, and the cab moved downtown at a decent clip.

"So how you know Phil?" Hauser asked.

"We met at Theatre 80—you know Theatre 80, down on Saint Mark's Place?"

"Yeah, down Saint Mark's Place." (Snuff.) "I been there. I think last time I saw, it was a Jeanette MacDonald, it was *Maytime,* one of those operettas."

"Yeah, so Phil and I kept running into each other down there and he told me he was starting his own job over at the Beth. He loves you, Frank, I mean it. He was just telling me last night about the whole Norwegian thing, what a gas it was talking to the Norwegian operators and all." Hauser laughed and snorted simultaneously. Dusty smiled.

"What're you getting downtown?"

"I gotta pick up a phone machine, a Sanyo." (Snuff.)

"Place on Cortlandt Street, Lexograph Hi Fi, you ever go there?"

"No, I get most of my stuff at Radio House."

Hauser's eyes went to slits and he gave one of his snorts, this one filled with derision. Dusty could tell he'd just lost a lot of points. "Radio House? You might as well go through garbage cans in Japan or England." (Snuff.) "BSR makes their turntables, fuckin' Panasonic subsidary makes the receivers." (Snuff.) "Don't even have equalizers."

Jesus, thought Dusty, I didn't mean to attack his family or anything. "I just go there for tapes now and then, a phone jack, stuff like that." Dusty retreated hastily from the offending position.

There was silence as Hauser gazed out the window. "So what's this deal?" he said, finally.

"I want you to tap someone's phone for me." The phrase hung melodramatically in the back seat of the cab. "Okay? I mean you can do that, right?'"

Hauser kept looking out the window. "Yeah, I can do that. The question is—" (Snuff.) "Why should I?"

"Hey, I'll pay you, Frank. Whatever. The thing is, there's information coming in on this phone that I gotta get. It might even be too late now." He wasn't going over. He had approached it too abruptly, hadn't used enough soft soap. He wanted to kick himself, hard. He backtracked.

"Listen, Frank, Phil told me there was no one even close to you with phones—he said they were alive to you, they were like your friends, that you practically made 'em jump through a hoop—" The cab stopped in a street teeming with people—Dusty paid the fare (three fifty-five, shit, and Hauser grunted gracelessly onto the sidewalk.

The store had very high ceilings, and the shelves were stacked with boxes containing pin jacks, alligator clips—every conceivable electronic attachment.

"Lenny here?" Frank asked the kid at the counter. Behind him was a doorway leading to the bench area of the shop.

"Yo. Hey, Lenny—" the kid called back. "Your friend's here."

A big, dark-haired guy rolled out from the back. He could have been Hauser's brother, except his hair was dark and thinning and Hauser's was sandy. Same type

and it's a self-service elevator, better yet. Instead of going up Dusty presses B for basement and goes down, down to the storerooms—one, two, three, four, five doors—all secured with new brass padlocks. Down to the green room, opposite the locks, papered with *Playboy* centerfolds (for Albert?). Down to the laundryroom, where a big economy-size box of Tide rests against the inside of a windowsill in the dim light from the courtyard above.

He'd arrived before five in case there was a super or someone who might have locked up the basement. Some apartment buildings had doors to the basement that were locked when the super wasn't there. Dusty was taking no chances.

By the green room, locked to a heating pipe with a big yellow chain, was a Peugeot ten-speed bike. Doe was always asking when she could get a hip bike like that, and he'd made up his mind to give her one in two years, when she was twelve. He wondered if she'd get to be twelve. Christ, I'll kill those bastards, so help me.

He rode the elevator back upstairs. Hauser was outside, smoking—just the thing for his sinus. "Frank!" he called, and Hauser turned, saw him in the doorway. Dusty smiled at affable Albert as he held the door for Frank and his attaché case. The indispensable attaché case.

And into the elevator. "You got the loot?" (Snuff.)

Dusty nodded. "You want it now?"

"Why not?" Dusty gave him five twenties, and they stepped out at the basement level.

"I was down here before," Dusty said, "but I didn't know what to look for."

Frank was examining the ceiling, and now he began walking past the storerooms, keeping his gaze up and to the right, past the green room with the centerfolds, and Dusty saw Frank was following a cable. He hadn't thought to look for a cable, and he would've missed it anyway, as it was painted the same dull beige as the ceiling.

The cable veered down just before the laundryroom into the top of an oblong cabinet about four feet high, set against the wall a few feet from the ground.

"Here we are," Frank said, setting his case on the floor. He squatted beside it heavily. From the case he drew a long-handled instrument that looked like a piano tuner's wrench. When he applied it to the door of the box, the door swung open, and Dusty realized it was a special key.

Inside, Dusty could see a series of terminals, in two parallel rows, running vertically down the rear wall of the box. On the inside of the door was a diagrammed key, marked by apartments and floor: 1A, 1B, 1C, and so on—two sets of terminals to a floor.

Frank reached into his case again and brought out two lengths of rubber-shielded cable which ended in a common tip, a Japanese-made pin jack. On the other end each cable culminated in a tiny steel horseshoe.

(Snuff.) "What's the apartment?" Frank asked.

"Twelve A."

Frank moved his finger down the key code inside the door until he came to 12A, then located the corresponding terminals. He drew a small, plastic-handled screwdriver from his inside jacket pocket, and loosened the screw of the first terminal just enough to allow the insertion of one of the little horseshoes. He retightened the screw. Then he repeated the operation on the second terminal and shut the door of the cabinet. The pin jack now hung from the bottom of the cabinet.

"You gonna sit here and monitor?" (Snuff.) "Or you wanna hook it up to tape?"

"Can I do both? I mean, can I monitor the tape?"

"Sure." From his case Hauser took a small Sony tape recorder and a cassette reel (C-90), which he placed in the machine. He plugged the pin jack into the input marked AUX. IN. at the back of the recorder. Reaching once more into his case, he extracted a pair of Koss headphones and plugged them into the AUX OUT. outlet. Then he turned on the recorder and extended the headphones to Dusty. "You're all set," he said.

Dusty took the headphones, which were shaped like a doctor's stethoscope. He placed the earpieces in his ears and heard nothing.

Hauser gave a characteristic snort. "You won't hear anything till the phone activates."

Dusty nodded.

"And you gotta leave the recorder on" (snuff) " 'cause the line's playing through the tape, y'understand? I could hook you up with just headphones" (snuff) "but you wouldn't get it on tape. So make sure you leave the recorder on, okay?"

Dusty nodded again.

"You can bring me the recorder and the phones on" (snuff) "Wednesday, with the rest of the loot, okay?"

"Okay. I'll see you Wednesday. I really 'preciate this, Frank."

"Hope you get what you want," said Hauser, and snorted his way into the elevator.

Dusty checked his watch. It was six twenty. He brought a chair from the laundryroom and sat with the recorder in his lap, the phones in his ears, watching the tiny reels spin inside the plastic window. Yeah, I hope I get what I want. Though it was entirely possible Maricot's call had come in sometime earlier, before Frank had set him up. It was entirely possible he was spending two hundred bucks for bupkes. And where am I gonna get that other hundred for Frank? He tucked his leg under him and stared at the Sony's metal casing, stared at the little short arrows that indicated FF or REW or STOP . . . and there was PLAY and RECORD and an extra button for PAUSE. . . .

The next thing he knew it was five past seven, and his leg was numb. He had fallen asleep in his chair. Gotta watch that, he thought, as he moved his leg and a thousand needles rose from his sole to his knee. Anh! He looked at the machine. The tape had stopped. In fact it was the automatic shutoff that had clicked him awake. He opened the machine, flipped the cartridge over, pressed PLAY and RECORD, and was about to try and get up on his numb leg when he heard the earphones come alive with presence. Someone was calling, there was the dull buzz of a ring, once, twice, and then he heard Syndee's voice.

"Hello, you have reached seven-nine-nine, oh-six-four-one, but no one is here right now. When you hear the beep tone, please leave your name and telephone number and the time of your call and I will get back to you. The beep takes a little while to come so please be patient. Thank you." There was silence for a few seconds and then the rising *beep* that only the Phone-Mate answering machine makes. Dusty waited tensely for the next voice.

"Oh, shit, Syndee, I wanted to talk to you. I hate these damn machines." It was a female, but not Maricot. "Listen, Miller's doesn't have any more, but they said they'll be getting them in soon. Um . . . shit, I really wanted to talk to you. Well, um . . . call me. I'll be home after eleven. Did you go to Don's party? Jerry said it was fantastic. I'm hanging up—call me after elev—" And the machine clicked off.

So. Syndee was out. He wondered whether that was going to affect anything Maricot might have to say. He got up and stretched his leg.

Between the hours of eight and twelve Syndee got one more call, from an older-sounding man who was confirming their date for Friday night. He was flying in from San Francisco. Dusty wondered idly whether Syndee did a little high-class tricking on the side.

The tape clicked off at twenty past twelve and Dusty was turning the cartridge over when he heard the elevator descending. Shit, it must be Albert. He'd forgotten about old Albert. Albert could cause trouble. Dusty pulled the phones out of his ears, got up, and placed them cautiously beside the recorder on the chair. He moved the chair silently into the deepest shadow he could find and quickly stationed himself in the darkened laundryroom.

He heard someone coughing, a wheezing cough, and he was sure now it was Albert. Then the elevator door sighed open, and Dusty could hear the doorman shuffle slowly along the hall to the green room. Those *are* Albert's centerfolds, the horny old bastard.

Albert took eleven minutes to do whatever he was doing in the green room (Jerking off? At his age?). Changing clothes, probably. Hurry up, you old fart. What if the call comes in? And it was at that moment Dusty realized he *hadn't turned the machine on* after he'd flipped the reel. With a panicky sense of "I'm gonna miss it," Dusty beelined back to the chair, pressed the PLAY and RECORD buttons, and heard the metallic music of Syndee's message in the headphones. *Someone was calling.* At this moment Albert stepped out of the green room. He had changed from his dark gray uniform into an old navy pea coat. He saw Dusty and his rheumy eyes widened with surprise.

"What you do here?"

"Shhh! Shhhh!" Dusty hissed. Syndee's message was nearly over.

"Not to shush. You no shush me!" cried Albert, and with a forceful swing of his arm he arced a blow at Dusty, who automatically ducked his head. Dusty watched in horror as Albert's arm connected with the headphone cord, knocking the jack out of the recorder.

"Goddamn you!" Dusty yelled, and pushed the old man viciously back into the green-room doorway, and even as he did so he had a fantasy vision of the old man's head cracking open on the doorjamb. No! he thought, no! And he wiped the blood and brains from his mind in time to see the old man scuttle down the hall and up the service stairs. You been seeing too many movies, Dusty told himself as he frantically reinserted the phones. Thank God the old fart didn't rip the recorder away from the terminal box. Jamming the earpieces back in his head, he heard no voice, but the presence of live air. It was the end of the receiving tape being played out. Dusty waited till the presence clicked off and pressed the button marked REW. He let it run for a count of five, stopped the machine, and was just about to push the PLAY button when he heard Albert yelling frantically upstairs. "Help, help!" the old man was crying. He had to get out of there. If the cops caught him tapping phone lines they could really put him away for a while and he'd never get to Dorothy.

Stuffing the headphones in his jacket pocket and carrying the Sony, he found his way to the service stairs (he didn't want to get trapped in the elevator) and raced up to the lobby. Cautiously, he stuck his head out. The old man was peering through the wrought-iron doors, obviously waiting for the police. Quickly, Dusty made his way across the lobby, grabbed the big door with his left hand, and tore it open. With his right hand he pulled Albert into the lobby away from him.

"Outta my way, old man, or you're dead."' Dusty stuck his hand in his jacket pocket, pushing the lining out with the earpiece of the headphones, hoping Albert would think he had a pistol.

Albert blinked uncertainly at him for a split instant, and then hurled himself on Dusty, crashing them both down the stone stoop. Shit, Dusty thought, even as he slid down the steps, this alta cocker didn't even *see* the fuckin' pistol, he's so blind.

"You see what happens!" Albert was yelling. "You see!" They were down on the street in a tangle of arms and legs.

I'm gonna have to clobber this guy, Dusty thought, and I don't know how to do it without hurting him. And then he heard the faint *rrrr* of a siren. Shit, somebody called the cops. And he scrambled to his feet but the old fucker was hanging on to his leg. Jesus Christ, do I kick him in the face? *Kick him in the face!* He drew his other leg back and this time Albert saw—he saw it fine. He realized Dusty's intention and instinct made him shield his face with both hands and Dusty felt the grip leave his leg and he had to hop backwards three, four times, but he didn't fall, he didn't fall and Albert was yelling, "Stop! stop!" even as he ran to West End Avenue. And as he climbed into the taxi he prayed, oh, how he prayed that what he needed was on the cassette.

11

In the cab he pressed the PLAY button, but the Sony refused to operate. He hit both REW and FF but something was jammed somewhere. Must've busted in the fight. Shit, now he was gonna have to repair Hauser's machine.

He tried to extract the cartridge—he could play it on his own deck at home—but the little window wouldn't open. Terrific. It won't play and it won't come out.

Upstairs in his apartment he took a screwdriver handle and carefully smashed the plastic window until he located the little spring that hinged the cover. He placed the cassette in his Panasonic and pressed the PLAY button.

"—ime of your call and I will get back to you." he heard. "The beep takes a little while to come so please be patient. Thank you." And then came the rising beep and Dusty held his breath.

The first thing he heard was a different presence, as if from a distance. then he heard a voice he knew very well. It was Maricot. "Hello, Syndee . . . listen, *chère amie,* call me collect when you get in, *d'accord?* Oh, it's *très très français ici.* Listen, I'm a wee bit high. *Le nombre, le nombre* . . . it's ahria code three-one-eight, and then it's . . . " At this point Maricot broke into giggles. Hurry up, Dusty urged her or the tape'll run out. "Ahria code three-one-eight, two-three-four . . . seven-four-seven-one, okay? I hahv to give you—" and then the tape clicked off.

Dusty's fist was clenched to his mouth. I got it, I got

it! No rumor, no bullshit—this was from the horse's mouth, baby. He played it over and wrote the number on the back of an envelope. Then he picked up the phone and dialed it, station to station.

A male voice answered after two rings. "Good morning, Shair'ton Tan Hahss," and Dusty thought, Holy mack'rel, Kingfish, we is in de deeeeep South.

"Yes, I've lost your address, could you give it to me please?"

"Be glay'ud to, sir. We're at tain twainty Pinhook, 'bout a mahl southwest on one eighty-two."

Dusty was writing it down. "Pinhook Avenue?"

"Pinhook Road, sir."

"And how far is that from New Orleans?"

" 'Bout eighty-fahv miles, sir. Can ah make a reservation for you?"

"No, thanks, I need to write somebody there. Tell me, what's the name of the town you're in?"

"Whah, Lafayette, sir. Named after the general."

"Thanks very much," said Dusty, and hung up. He wanted to ask which was the nearest airport, but he couldn't afford to arouse even the slightest suspicion. He got up and brushed his teeth, and in the mirror his face was a mask of triumph. I've *got* them, the bastards.

It was ten past one as he slipped into bed, thinking about the Sheraton Town House in Lafayette, Louisiana, and how to get there. Okay, say airfare is two hundred, and car rental is another hundred, and room and food for a coupla days is another sixty, and return ticket for the kid is another hundred—that's four sixty, say five hundred which is five hundred more than I got. Christ, I wouldn't give this spot to a leopard. Money, money, money, and now I owe Hauser another hundred plus a fuckin' Sony. And in the midst of this he felt his stomach start up again. Oh, Jesus God, not again.

He turned on the bedside lamp, popped the cap off his Valium vial, shook out five milligrams, and swallowed it down at the bathroom sink. Stay cool, he told himself, it's just gas. He got down on the bedroom floor, supporting himself on his knees and elbows, sticking his butt in the air, a trick his mother, of all people, had taught him. To bring up the gas, make you fart it out. I wonder, should I see Dr. Zahm about this and that goddamned headache? That's all I need now, right? To go into chemotherapy or something. He felt the bubble come up, finally, and, after a few more minutes, he was able to close his eyes

He dreamed he was in his Volvo, driving along an unidentified back road, in dappled sunshine, very peaceful, very pastoral. The road slipped beneath the wheels and the trees rushed by, but he had the feeling he wasn't covering any distance; it was like being in one of those amusement park racers where the road comes at you from a screen and you get points for each obstacle you manage to miss. He had the feeling he was looking for something but he didn't know what, and he just kept driving and driving and not getting anywhere, and then he stepped on the accelerator and the car went from seventy to forty—that's not supposed to happen, something was impeding the forward motion, dragging the car slower. The back of the car felt heavy—was it something in the trunk? And he got out of the car (while it was moving) and ran beside it till he reached the trunk. Yes, I know, you can't do that, but that's what he did, like running on a treadmill, and he put the key in the trunk of the Volvo and sprung the lid, and inside, as it lifted, he saw the heads of two animals, the severed, bloody necks of a black chicken and a white goat—eyes glazed and shining in stricken, helpless attitude. And occupying the crowning position, perched atop the spare tire (which in the Volvo was anchored vertically on the right), was *Dorothy's disembodied head!* And she was laughing! Her eyes swept the blood-spattered trunk, and as she drank in the hideous carnage she said "he, he, he" in her characteristic giggle—"He, he, he," which made it even more chilling. "He, he, he. He, he, he. HE, HE, HE—"

The phone rang and he started out of sleep, shaking. Thank God, he thought, as he swam upward from the devastation of this terrible image. Thank God the phone is ringing, thank God I'm not asleep anymore, and he fumbled for the phone, and it was Rossie, Dorothy's homeroom teacher.

"Miss Ross? Oh, yes, sure . . . ah . . . how are you?"

"I am quite well, thank you." She spoke with a Scandinavian accent—she was from Helsinki or somewhere. "I heup I deun't wake you."

"No, no, not at all." He threw extra energy into his voice, the way you do when you're trying to convince someone you've been up for years. "What can I do for you?"

"We were joost wondering about Dorothy—whether maybe she had caught the fleu pehaps. When she wasn't here yesterday, I thought I weuld give you a call if she wasn't here again today."

"Right, right. Miss Ross, Dorothy had to take a trip with her mother. But it's really nice of you to call and ah . . . inquire."

"Do yeu have any idea when she'll be back, Mr. Greener? I'd like to be able to tell the other cheuldren." What a sweetie-pie Rossie was. "Sure, Miss Ross, you tell the kids Dorothy'll be back by Monday." There was a tiny pause, and Dusty could tell Monday wasn't soon enough for Miss Ross.

"Very weul, Mr. Greener. Euf yeu speak to her, tell her we've hung her drawing up with the others, euven theugh it's not finished."

"You bet I will, Miss Ross. And thank you again for calling, very much." Boy, that's a teacher, he thought as he shaved and dressed. I wonder if she calls Marvin Berman's father if Marvin's out a coupla days.

And then he remembered he had to get five hundred and sixty dollars.

He pondered the possibilities. There was nothing coming from Leonard, not till after the weekend, anyway. Phil, maybe. Ah, he thought, Phil has no money. Arline. Now that's an idea. He might catch her in the office, if she wasn't at court. He dialed, and she was there, but unluckily, she was in a bind herself.

"I would if I could, Dusty, but, you know, Gerry had a relapse—"

"Oh, no, Christ, I didn't know that."

"Yes, and the hospital bills are just incredible. Well, you can imagine, even with Blue Cross. I'm taking out a second mortgage on the house. I have to. Gerry's just sick about it."

Gerry's just sick, period, Dusty thought as he hung up. He dialed Delta Airlines and booked a seat on both flights out of Kennedy to New Orleans that night; the six thirty and the one at two fifty in the morning. Jesus. Somehow he was going to be on one of them. Somehow.

He went to the étagère and unscrewed the speaker

wires from the Marantz receiver. He pulled out the turntable leads, and then reached down behind and yanked the plug out of the wall. With determination in his eyes he took the machine downstairs to the pawnshop on Fifty-fourth and Eighth Avenue.

The man in the shop began shaking his head almost before Dusty put the thing down on the glass-topped counter. "Another receiver? Take it away—I have a roomful of them."

"Don't gimme that," Dusty barked aggressively. "I paid four hundred and forty-nine dollars for this thing. It's a Marantz." The guy didn't stop shaking his head. Dusty wanted to hit him.

"All right then, screw you. I'll take it to Sterling." Sterling was the next hockshop down the avenue, on Fifty-first. Dusty lifted the machine from the counter.

"I couldn't give you more than fifty dollars for it."

"Bullshit. You'll give me two hundred."

The man put his hand on the machine at arm's length and studied it with the expression of a doctor pulling down the skin below your eye. Without saying anything, he walked through a swinging door at the far end of the counter, up where the shop had brass-barred windows for the exchange of money. Dusty heard the low murmur of voices, and somebody said Marantz and the model number. He looked around the pawnshop. Old Admiral TV sets. Bell & Howell projectors. Hanging from the ceiling were dozens of guitars; he saw the name Gretsch on several. And behind the counter, in three glass cases, was a selection of small arms—pistols, revolvers and automatics.

The man came back. Morris Carnovsky on a bad day, thought Dusty.

"Fifty," said the man, nodding.

"The hell with you," Dusty said. "I'm keeping it. Whaddaya want for that little twenty-two target pistol?"

"You bring in your license, we'll talk about it, all right?"

"You're a wise motherfucker, aren't you?" Dusty spat at him, and took his receiver back out to the avenue.

He brought it back upstairs and irritably began packing his overnight case. He threw in a change of socks and underwear, his toilet things, a Lacoste T-shirt in case it was warm, his cavalry twill slacks, his light Cardin turtleneck, and his Adidas running sneakers, not that he ran —they were just hip shoes. He put on his McCreedy & Schreiber boots, his jeans, a body shirt, and a sweater, and his leather jacket, whch was beginning to tear at the right armpit. He stuffed his checkbook in the back pocket of his jeans, and then he called his service. It took them seven rings to pick up at *their own number!* Christ. He really ought to get one of those machines, the kind Syndee had. They paid themselves off in about four months.

"Six four oh three, just a moment."

"Never mind just a moment, you know you didn't pick up till the seventh ring?"

"Who's this?"

"This is the late, great Dusty Greener, Marie, and you girls better get your ass in gear or I'm quitting this stupid service. I'll get a machine."

"You have no messages, Dusty."

"Thanks a lot. Listen, I'm going away for a coupla days. I'll check in with you tomorrow night, okay? Put a note in the box, 'out of town.' " He decided definitely when he got back to cancel the service and get a machine. It'll give me something else I can't hock, he thought sourly.

He went to the deli and cashed twenty-five with the Fat Man—walking around money. Fuck it, he thought. I'll give Delta a bum check if I have to. There was one more ace in his hand. Cheryl, down at the Beth Co-op.

It was about seven when he walked in (he'd waited for some loot to pile up in the till), and he saw Cheryl smile behind her cage. "You're getting to be a regular."

"Cheryl, listen, I know you helped me out once this week already, but I'm in a jam. I need a hundred cash right now. Can you do it for me?"

Cheryl's face broke into a pained grin. "Oh, Dusty, Angie came by this afternoon and collected a whole bunch of cash. I doubt if I have even—" she rummaged through the drawer—"thirty dollars in here. Just enough to make change." She saw desperation cloud his face. "I have about fifteen, will that help? We could prob'ly scrape together about fifty."

But Dusty was already making his way out. "Thanks, Cheryl," he called back. "Thanks anyway."

12

He was drinking Dry Sack over ice in a gay bar, a joint called The Painted Pony on Eighty-fourth and Third Avenue. It was nine fifteen and he kept asking himself, What am I doing here, how is this gonna help me get my loot?

He had left the Beth Co-op empty-handed, carrying his overnight bag down Bleecker to Sheridan Square, hammering his head for anyone in the Village who could help him. He'd wandered down Christopher to Eighth Street and then east, past the Art movie theater, and the Marboro Bookstore, and the old Bon Soir and Number One Fifth Avenue, and the next thing he knew he was at Astor Place. It was quarter to eight already, which meant he'd missed the six-thirty flight and would have to make the two fifty. He still didn't have any loot. Sure, I can pay the airfare with a bum check, he thought, but once I get to Louisiana, what then? What about car rental, food, his motel?

He had found himself on the 101 bus, riding uptown on Third Avenue. Past Movie Row at Sixtieth Street, past Oscar's. For some reason he got off at Eighty-second and started walking uptown. I'll tour Eighty-sixth Street, he figured, and something will happen, something will come to me. When he reached the little bar on Eighty-fourth, the dryness in his throat became unbearable, and he needed a glass of wine. As soon as he walked in he knew it was a gay bar by the stack of magazines on the jukebox. *Michael's Thing.* What a name for a magazine. There were stools around the piano bar and a hand-lettered sign that advertised a pianist, Dick Haddy, Tuesday through Saturday. Sunday was talent night.

By the jukebox was a series of hooks that acted as a coatroom, but it was completely exposed. Dusty kept his overnight bag with him, sticking it under one of the stools at the piano bar as he sat down. He leaned his forearms on the Naugahyde cushion that buffed the circumference of the piano-shaped bar. The cushion had been torn in several places and patched with masking tape.

A young, willowy black queen came over and batted his eyes. "Hi, I'm Joee. May I help you?" Dusty realized this was the waiter.

"Yeah, I'll have a Dry Sack on the rocks." A place like this wouldn't have any wine to speak of. He saw Joee, back at the bar, ring a little bell, the kind you call bellboys with. *Front.* The bartender came to Joee from the other end of the L-shaped bar, and Dusty watched Joee, in pantomime, order his Dry Sack. What the fuck am I doing here? he asked himself. I gotta get to Louisiana. He looked at the bar. There were three or four guys drinking beer or Scotch and they were all looking at him.

Joee brought his drink and lingered. Dusty saw he was wearing a wig—black, tight, and curly. "When's the entertainment start?" he asked.

"Depends what you're looking for," Joee replied, and dropped his eyes demurely.

Joee gave new meaning to the word coquette. Dusty couldn't help grinning. "How about a giraffe and two mice?"

"Darling, where do you think you are, Tijuana?"

"What's this guy Haddy do?"

"Anything you want, for a price."

"I can see I'm not gonna get a straight answer outta you, Joee."

"Darling, you're not gonna get a straight anything *out* of me. Try another direction." Joee flounced off and the jukebox began Streisand's record of "How Lucky Can

to the front door and vestibule entrances where the mailboxes were. That's where I'll do it, Dusty decided. I'll get him into the vestibule. Or maybe I should wait till we're inside the door. Except what about the neighbors on the first floor—what if they hear something? Schmuck, this is New York, he told himself, nobody will hear anything.

Paul stopped before 232 East Eighty-third Street, and as the moment drew near Dusty wasn't sure he could do it—no, that wasn't it, he really didn't *want* to do it.

"Listen, Paul," he said, in a final effort to avoid this, "do you have five hundred dollars? I mean, where you can get your hands on it, like in cash?"

Paul looked at him strangely, but with total comprehension. It was amazing how sober people got when money was the subject.

"Wait a minute . . . 'm I being hustled here?"

"I'm serious about this, Paul. I need five hundred dollars. Now if you can give me the cash I won't have to hurt you." Dusty said it very straight and level, but he saw Paul decide to take it as a gag.

Paul smiled his dribbling smile. "C'mon upstairs and we'll talk about it," he said, as he climbed the three steps to the vestibule.

"Okay," said Dusty, and as Paul dug in his pocket for his keys, Dusty clamped his hands together tightly, raised them high above his head, and brought them down with all his force on the back of Paul's neck.

The effect was astounding: the impact of the blow slammed Paul downward about three feet and sideways into the corner of the vestibule. Dusty saw instant blood on the man's upper lip and realized he had hit his mouth on the doorknob. The red smear was spreading rapidly all over Paul's lip and Dusty looked away from the stricken eyes—eyes that suddenly realized this was no joke, no hustle, this was for real.

Dusty moved in on his victim and crushed him to the wall with his body, pinning his arms with both hands. He looked down, slipped his right foot between Paul's legs, and brought his knee up with a fierce jerk. Paul's eyes widened and he cried out in pain and Dusty thought, Shit, why didn't I cover his mouth before I did that, and Paul was trying to bend double to reach his throbbing groin, but Dusty's body was in the way.

Now Dusty withdrew and Paul slid to the floor, clutching his crotch. Dusty bent swiftly to him and reached inside his jacket, searching for Paul's wallet. He spoke in a harsh whisper.

"I'm in a jam—otherwise I wouldn't do this, you gotta believe me." He found the wallet. It was black pigskin with little gold corners on it. "If you'd given me the loot when I asked you Paul. I *asked* you." Dusty found what he wanted: an American Express card and another verifier (they always wanted two pieces of identification)—a Chase Manhattan Convenience Card. He held them up to Paul's face.

"I'm taking your credit card and your bank card, Paul. I need to use them for about three days. When I'm through with them I'll send 'em back, okay? Okay, Paul?" Paul nodded as the blood flooded steadily into his mouth from his torn upper lip. Dusty seized Paul by the throat and sat him roughly up against the wall.

"And gimme your keys, you fucker." He began slapping Paul's pockets. He was angry at Paul for making him do this, and he knew that was irrational, yes, but the anger helped, made him effective.

"Gimme your keys!" he barked, and Paul was scared now, really frightened, and he reached in his pocket, hoping Dusty wasn't going to kill him, and pulled out his keys, which were on a sterling silver ring. Dusty snatched them angrily.

"All right, you fucker. I'm throwing these keys under a car on this block." That would keep him occupied for an hour or so, and Dusty could be out of there on the two-fifty flight.

"Don't call the police, fucker, I'm warning you. Just think of this as a loan—I'm sending these cards back in three days, and I'll pay you back the bread when I get back. I just need it now, okay?"

Paul stared at him, not daring to move. Dusty pushed Paul's head back with the heel of his hand. Paul's eyes went sick with fear.

"Answer me, you fucker, okay?" Paul nodded, and Dusty rose to his feet, snatched his overnight bag, and fled down the steps into the night.

~ 13 ~

If she had to rate it on a scale from one to ten, Dorothy would give herself a five for bravery, but she was very scared. It had been okay till last night, but last night they had made her drink that shitty stuff and now she was scared, really scared. The stuff had made her crazy, made her silly and stupid, flopping all over the couch and giggling like a hyena. It was kind of like the dentist that time Dr. Oxenfeld gave her laughing gas and she had those crazy dreams, except this stuff was twenty times as strong as laughing gas, and there was that really scary feeling of being out of your body watching everything and at the same time knowing you were in your body but not being able to get the two feelings together.

The trouble was, she almost liked it. It was dizzy, but it was funny sometimes, like when Mommy and Raoul took the cushions from the couch and then played catch with them, tossing the cushions real hard and trying to knock everybody down. She really tried to knock Raoul down. She wished he was dead, the retard. He had no right to touch her, grabbing her up in his arms like he was her real daddy and doing all that phony disgusting goochy goo stuff. At the same time there was this terrific kind of, um, feeling. She had tried to squirm out of his grip and he had held her tighter, and she could feel his strength pinning her to him, and for a moment she had an inkling of what went on inside the bedroom when they closed the door. She knew they were going to do it again, that night—make her drink that shitty stuff again, after Raoul came back from Avery Island. And she thought of the note she kept in her panties, next to her butt, the note with her home phone on it that she was just waiting to slip to Mr. Farnon at the desk. Mr. Farnon liked her, and she knew he'd make the call for her if she could only find a way to slip it to him. They made sure one of them was always around so she couldn't make the call herself, otherwise she'd be on that phone so fast. . . .

Mommy was in the bedroom now, answering the phone, arranging something for Raoul the Retard. She heard her mother say he should be back around four o'clock.

She had to get that note to Mr. Farnon soon—they were moving out of here today, that's what Raoul had said. They were going someplace else, to Avery Island, which was in another parish. That's what they call the towns here, parishes.

The Retard was going to work for the McIlhenny Company on an oil rig "off the Gulf," and he was out right now arranging things with somebody named Lavo, and Dorothy knew Dusty had to get here quick, before she disappeared.

That's how it felt. That's how it felt when you drank that shitty stuff, as if part of you were disappearing and the part that was left wasn't really you but someone else, or even some*thing* else, what? An animal? *Something.*

And Mommy had the cha-cha. Frankie was right, she'd had it all along—the drum too, the assator, and last night, when they made her drink the crazy stuff, the Retard had played the assator with his hands, like a conga drummer, and Mommy had shaken the cha-cha deliberately once, twice, thrice, in a slow, kind of sexy way, like those hypnotist guys on TV, and then she'd danced with her, beckoned her out to the middle of the room and danced with her on the carpet, and she'd been Mommy again, beautiful Mommy, just for those few minutes when they danced together. Oh, when Mommy danced there was nothing like it in the world, and, gee, how she'd wished Frankie coulda been here to dance with Mommy, to feel his bare feet on the thick carpet, to hold her. She knew Frankie liked Mommy the best—he was just crazy about her, damn her, damn her, damn her! It was all her fault, Apricot's—she ruined everything!

The door swung open and Raoul came into the room. "Hey, ladies. Poppa's home."

Doe looked at him levelly. "You're not my poppa."

Raoul cocked a pistol finger at her. "Let's put it this way, *poquito*. Right now I'm the guy puts the roof over your head and the food in your mouth. So be nice to me, okay?" He strode inside and dropped down on the bed next to Maricot, folding his arms behind his head.

"I found her, baby. Down in Avery Island. I told her we'd be moving in tonight. I hadda give her two bills in front. I wish you'da been there, to haggle with her, like you do. Creole lady, you know? You coulda got round her in French, I know you could."

Maricot was alert. "What kind of place does she have?"

"Listen, don't start salivatin'—she don't have nothin' fancy. It's the ground floor of a house. There's a bedroom and a kitchen, and a Castro in the living room, and it's fifty a week, and it's where we live now—twenty-six Duloyne Street—so start packin'. I told her we'd move in tonight."

Maricot's eyes were gleaming. "Does it have—?"

"Yeah, yeah, it's got a big back yard, she's got all the supplies, and wait'll you see the tree. There's this big old oak covers the whole yard like an umbrella. A real masterpiece, you know? Made me want to go into forestry. I mean it, it's not till you get out of that rotten city and see something like that tree . . . " He sat up and took a glassine pouch of grass from the night table. Expertly he spilled it into a one point five paper, licked it, and spread saliva on it with his finger.

"Did that guy call? Fournier?" he asked Maricot.

"Yes, lahv. I told him you'd be bahck at four."

"Didn't you get his number?"

"He didn't seem to think he should leave it with me."

"Oh, shit, Maricot. I gotta get in touch with him." His palm beat an irritated tattoo on the chenille bedspread. He lit up the joint, inhaled deeply, and passed it to Maricot. She shook her head. "Not now. And I wish you wouldn't either."

Raoul's chest caved in with a laugh. "Oh, is that the truth? Since when?"

"Since we're driving, and we hahv someone else we're responsible for." She indicated the living room with her head.

In the living room Dorothy was slipping the paper back into her panties; "26 Dulane St.," she had written, "Avery Iland." She looked up as her mother came through the door, her peignoir flowing about her. Maricot loved to laze the day away in bed and then get dressed and play at night. She kneeled beside the couch. A pillow, a sheet, and a blanket were stacked meticulously at the foot of the couch.

"Sweetness, come in and help us pahck."

"Awwww . . . do I have to?" She read it like a line in a play, acting the bored kid, pretending there was nothing going on, pretending she wasn't desperately seeking a way to get that note to Mr. Farnon.

Dorothy knew Maricot's habit of leaving money for the maid. Maybe she could get to perform that chore for her mother and hide her note under the bills. Or wait—a better idea!

"I'll be in in a minute," she said, rubbing her eyes, as if she needed the time to wake up from a nap. Maricot went back in the bedroom, and Dorothy opened the drawer of the writing desk, beneath the big TV set. She took the long, hotel-style, black ballpoint and a sheet of blue and white stationery from the drawer. "Mr. Farnon," she wrote. "Please call my father, Dusty Greener at area code 212 CO 5–6624 and tell him I am at 26 Dulane st. in Avery Iland, Luisana." Then she folded the paper, and on the front she wrote "FOR MISTER FARNON" in big capitals. The message she had written in the round, cursive script Rossie was teaching them, making sure all the loops were big enough, and all the stems were the same length. She stuck the note under her T-shirt and stepped into the bathroom.

"Mommy, do you and Raoul have all your stuff from the bathroom?" She opened the medicine chest and placed everything in the bowl of the sink—shaving cream, deodorant stick, razor, tube of Crest. She took the note from under her shirt, opened the Crest, and squeezed a strip of the light blue paste onto the back of the paper. She stuck the note to the rear wall of the medicine cabinet with Mister Farnon's name clearly in view for the maid to see. She had to fold the lower edge of the page to make it fit, but that was okay—it made it more noticeable. The maid was sure to spot it. Now all she had to do was keep Mommy and the Retard away from the medicine chest.

She gathered the toiletries into her hands and went to the bedroom. Apricot had her three cases open—two on the floor, one on the bed. She stuck the deodorant stick and the razor into the side of the case on the bed, and as she did she saw Mommy had packed her sequin top, the one she always wore in *Sweet Charity*. Was Mommy going to work down here? And there was that Ortho stuff—she'd asked about that stuff before. For some reason Mommy didn't like talking about it. It was part of the dirty stuff. Maybe it was part of the bleeding.

And sticking out of the elastic pouch in the lid of the case was a radish. A radish—now that was curious. She pulled the radish out and saw that it was joined to a poato, and the potato had chunks of carrot on each side for arms, but no legs. It was a little vegetable doll—weird, weird-o-rama. The radish had been pierced through by something pointed (Mommy's hatpin?) where the ears would have been, also the base of the potato, at what might correspond to the small of the back. Maybe it was a prop. Maybe it went with the Ortho stuff.

She started guiltily. Maricot was smiling at her from across the bed. Perhaps Dorothy was coming around after all, Maricot was thinking. She'd been such a bad girl on the flight down—cranky and kicking and simply ungovernable, trying to convince the stewardess she was being kidnapped. Raoul had had to be rather harsh with her then. But now, after the past two days, Maricot thought, maybe she's starting to come around.

"I got it all, I cleaned everything out of the bathroom." Dorothy wanted to say, You don't have to go back in there, but she knew that would sound suspicious. She was even sorry she'd said, I cleaned out everything—that was laying it on a little heavy, right? Economy, right, Frankie? See, I'm learning, she thought. And I'm trying not to say "you know" so much. Oh, please, please come and get me, she pleaded silently. If you'll come get me, I'll never say "you know" again, I promise. Only come and get me before they make me drink the shitty stuff again, and I get all dizzy and do something bad. She had that feeling very strongly—that Mommy and the Retard were gonna make her do something bad when she was dizzy and crazy from drinking the shitty stuff.

"Dahling, may I borrow your derriere?" Maricot put her hand on Raoul's boot, and Dorothy felt the unhealthy electricity that always crackled around the room when they touched, these two. The Retard came and kneeled on the first suitcase, his weight forcing the lid down on top of Mommy's gowns. Mommy didn't wear dresses, she wore Gowns. She didn't wear jeans, she wore Slacks. She didn't wear blouses or sweaters, she wore Tops. Dorothy watched Maricot put the rest of the toilet stuff into the third suitcase.

"I guess we're leaving now, hunh, Mommy?"

"Yes, angel."

Raoul spun the car keys around on his finger. "What time is that guy calling back? Four?"

"He said four, lahv."

"It's five fifteen." Raoul looked at his watch. "Shit."

"I'm hungry," Dorothy whined. Let's get going, she thought, let's get them out of here.

"My baby," Maricot cooed, "we'll give you some dinner ahs soon ahs we get to our new house." She turned to Raoul. "How long a drive is it, lahv?"

Raoul spun the keys impatiently. "Half an hour, maybe forty minutes. Shit. I gotta get in touch with this guy."

Dorothy knew why this guy was so important. He was going to give Raoul a lot of money for that white stuff, the stuff she had seen him suck into his nose through a dollar bill! He had a whole bag of it. He called it Stash, and he kept it under his bowling ball, all flattened out in a pouch in the case. Isn't that wild? When they got off the plane in New Orleans, Raoul had been very worried the baggage people had maybe lost his bowling ball and Dorothy couldn't figure out why that ball was so important until she learned the secret.

"How much money is that guy gonna give us?" asked Dorothy.

Raoul's eyes crinkled in amusement. "What's this 'us' business, big shot?"

"How much—a lot?"

"Enough to live on till our ship comes in, anyway."

Dorothy saw her mother throw Raoul a murderous

glance, the kind of look that said, *That's enough. Stop it right now.*

"When's that gonna be?"

"I don't really know, sweetheart, a month, two months." Raoul was obviously relishing some private joke, for he smiled very engagingly. "Wouldn't you say, lover?"

Maricot was looking at Raoul as if she could kill him. He had apparently touched a forbidden topic. "Come on, Dorothy, it's time to go," she said firmly, and Raoul sort of snickered as he picked up the suitcases, carried them out to the living room, and returned to the bedroom.

"Can I leave the money, Mommy? For the maid?" She tried to keep the eagerness out of her voice. Maricot fished in her purse and drew out two bills, a five and a single. She handed them to Dorothy absently. She was absolutely furious at Raoul, Dorothy saw, for something, and when she was like this, you better watch out.

Dodo sprinted into the living room with the bills, over to the big teardrop lamp on the little round table by the window, as far from her mother as she could get. Quickly, stealthily, she stuffed her hand inside her jeans, felt under her panties, and brought out the second note, which she placed under the two bills. She put the whole stack under the lamp, making sure the money covered the notepaper. She bounced innocently to the door.

"I'll carry the bowling ball," she said.

"You'll do no such thing, smahtie-pahnts. You come with me while we check out."

They started down the hall to the lobby. Raoul passed them on his way back for the last two cases. "Meetcha in the wagon," he said, and found himself puffing slightly. Shit, carrying a coupla lousy suitcases wasn't gonna wind him. He had other things to worry about—like that guy Fournier and his twelve hundred bucks. He was sacrificing a stash worth maybe fifteen, but this was needed cash, and besides, soon they were gonna be really rich, soon as they fixed Dorothy up and sent her back to Dusty. After that it was only a matter of time.

He looked around the deserted suite. He'd had to spring for a suite so they could ball in private, but it was worth it. Anytime you could have Maricot it was worth it. Whatever it cost in time, money, energy, lying, dealing, stealing, kidnapping—you name it—she was truly the best he'd ever had, no crap. And, Dios! when he'd found out about the loot! Wow, what a plan. At first he thought she was coming unhinged, you know? But after she'd worked a few numbers on him, he was almost ready to believe her. That Allocaine—phew, man, that was unbelievable—she'd almost made him walk out the window, *out the fuckin' window*. He had just set one foot after the other. He knew he was doing it. His mind was wide open but he was powerless, there was nothing he could do—he just kept walking and walking toward the open window, and when he'd put both legs over the sill and set his butt on the ledge, and Twenty-third Street was down there three fuckin' flights below him, he heard her say, And now if I tell you to push yourself off you will do it . . . and there was no sound but the wind faint in his ears and the buses coughing down there and he had waited, primed, ready for the word from her, the word he'd expected, the word that said go, push, do it—it seemed inevitable. But there was no word . . . only the wind and the buses, and finally she said, I have more fun with you alive, my lahv—come take me to bed. He had thought about that night a lot.

Of course, this voodoo number was too much. That was just plain bullshit. But he was going along with it, to keep her happy. Sure, what the hell, carve up the potatoes and the carrots, drag the drum around, get her a house with a back yard.

He saw the drum in the corner and slung it under his arm. He was about to pick up the two final suitcases when the open bathroom door caught his attention. I bet she forgot to steal the soap, he thought. Whenever he was in a motel, he always tossed the extra couple of cakes into his case.

They were usually in the medicine chest.

like Columbus Avenue—family stalls, you know. Bodegas. One'll sell fruit, one'll sell meat, but from what I could see, that meat's been hangin' a long time. A *long* time. We better stop in New Iberia." He glanced over at her and caught her expression of distaste. "Baby, listen, this here's the real backwoods. Now we knew it goin' in and we agreed, someplace completely isolated—"

"That's enough, Raoul."

For the second time that day Dorothy saw her mother silence Raoul, and she wondered, as she had begun to more and more, what this strange power was her mother seemed to have over people? Not people . . . men. Was it from being beautiful? Did being beautiful give you the right to tell people to shut up? Dorothy didn't know if she was going to be beautiful or not, but if she was, she was never going to be so rude to people, to treat them like . . . like they were dirt. That was no way to be. A person still has feelings, even if they're saying something you don't like.

They stopped in New Iberia and pulled into the back of the A&P, a big one. Dorothy noticed there were shopping carts in the parking lot. Wow, what a good idea. Roll your food right up to your car.

"We oughta have that in New York, Mommy." she said, as Raoul turned off the ignition.

"What's thaht, angel?"

"Shopping carts that go in the parking lot."

"What do you feel like eating, sweetness?"

"Dorothy, you come with me." Raoul had opened their door. We'll find something." He put his hand on Maricot's thigh. "Anything special you need?"

"Yes, get me a Maybelline Black Velvet eyebrow pencil. Dorothy knows."

Inside the market Raoul yanked a cart out of the stack. "Hey, Dorothy, you listen to me now, all right?" He sounded like that guy Marlon Brando that Frankie always imitated. "I wasn't kidding in the car. If I want to, I can make it very rough for you." She watched him mistrustfully. What did he want?

"But I can be a nice guy, too, you know?" He patted his pocket, the pocket where he'd put the note to Mr. Farnon. She started to roll the cart down the first aisle, but he gave a deft kick with his boot, and turned the front wheels into the shelves.

"Hey, Dorothy," he said, and his voice carried an unmistakable warning. "I mean it. You listen to me now, all right?" It wasn't a question, it was a command. He wasn't kidding.

"All right," she whispered.

"Okay, look, you're not supposed to know this, but in a week we're sending you home." Dorothy blinked. She didn't know whether to believe him or not. He squatted down to her level on his haunches.

"So you behave yourself for a week. That's all you have to worry about, okay?" He was looking at her, waiting for a verbal acknowledgment. What could she do? He had all the trading cards. She decided to go underground with her resistance.

"Okay, Raoul. It's a deal. I'll be a good girl. Can we have hamburgers?"

He rose to his feet. "Sure, hon, anything you want." She saw him nod satisfaction at her acquiescence. Yeah, she smiled inwardly. He thinks.

They wheeled two shopping bags back to the car. Raoul had been very careful about what they'd bought, reading the label on everything to make sure it was natural and unadulterated. He'd purchased two plastic gallons of Deer Park spring water, some wheat germ, and tomatoes and onions and avocados, though he'd complained they probably weren't organically grown and had spray on them.

He had insisted on Dorothy's picking out a lot of household items—Brillo pads, and paper towels, and a sponge —a lot of that stuff. Dorothy knew this was supposed to make her feel they were all one big happy family.

Okay, she could play the game. Carrying the lighter bag, she took it from the cart and placed it in the open rear of the flat-bed wagon, next to a red gasoline can with a silver spout. She wondered idly if the rental company supplied that or if Raoul got it special. And why, come to think of it, did Raoul rent a wagon like this instead of a smaller car? She knew he was worried about money, and a smaller car would've been cheaper. Maybe this was the only car the company had left. That happened sometimes. Frankie had told her once about renting a compact in California, but when he got there they didn't have any more compacts and they had to give him a big Chrysler for the same price and he drove around like a king.

She climbed back in the seat with a big manufactured

smile. "Mommy, guess what we're having for dinner? Hamburgers!"

They passed a place called Erath, and the road narrowed from four lanes to two, and then, as they bypassed Avery Island, even the two lanes got smaller—there was just barely room for two cars—and whenever someone came along the opposing lane, Raoul had to slow down. They passed through a kind of small settlement. You couldn't call it a real town—there was a Gulf station and a bar, and that was it—not even a five-and-ten. Dorothy looked for the bodegas Raoul had spoken of, but all she could see were two broken-down storefronts, with some black people hanging around, and then it was much darker. And it wasn't just that it was six o'clock—they were on a dirt road now, and these big gigantic trees were blocking out the last of the sunlight. The trees were beautiful, and they smelled of a green, piny freshness, but they hung over the road looking kind of scary, like the trees in Walt Disney that reached out to grab you. "Aren't these trees a gas?" said Raoul, his eyes shifting from left to right.

"What are they?" asked Dorothy.

"Oaks and cypresses. They knock me out. You know they've got a jungle garden down here—you can take a boat out on the Bayou Teche and see some dynamite wildlife. Flamingos and pelicans—all kindsa animals."

"And alligators, right?"

Raoul nodded. "Oh, you can see a few alligators, don't worry. And they can see you, so you better be a good girl, know what I mean?" He gave Dorothy a wink, but she was pretty sure Raoul would do it, too—feed her to an alligator if she was a bad girl. She remembered how he'd almost taped up Gina's eyes. Uch, the Retard, he was horrible.

Raoul made a right turn, and now the road had a rise in it, right in the middle. She could hear the top of the rise scrape the bottom of the wagon every so often—it made the gas can rattle around, and she thought if there were a lot of heavy stuff in the back you could get stuck out here. The cypress branches brushed the side of the car with whispery fingers, and she was glad Mommy was sitting near the window. She didn't want to be touched by those trees. And Raoul turned on the lights and Dorothy could see the house at the end of this puny road and at the same time she heard thunder. Thunder, as if the house were being announced by the malevolent rumble of death.

"Clouding over," said Maricot.

"More than that, according to Farnon," Raoul added. "He said we got here just in time for the monsoon season." As if to confirm this, the rumble sounded again.

"Ah, fuck it," said Raoul. "What difference does it make? We're here." He stepped out of the wagon, onto the grass.

"It could make a lot of difference," Maricot said mysteriously, and opened the door on the passenger side.

Dorothy sat very still in her seat. She had the feeling that if she got out, she would be adrift on an unfamiliar sea, and it made her uneasy. In the car she was still safe.

"Come on, lahv." Maricot reached in and pulled Doe's forefinger with an impatient tug.

Dorothy stared through the windshield at the house. It was a one-story wooden house, painted white, with a porch running around it. Dorothy could see touches of white again at the windows, and she guessed they were curtains. The house seemed to have been set into a clearing hollowed out by chopping the oaks and the cypresses back, but the shivery, low-swinging branches threatened to brush you with every billow of wind, and the wind was coming up now. The trees seemed to want to reclaim the area; it was like they kept coming in closer when you weren't looking, like playing "May I." If you caught them moving they had to stop, but the minute you turned your back again . . .

As she watched, the door of the house opened, and a figure scurried down the steps to meet them. Dorothy could see it was a woman, could see she was black, because in the dusk her eyes and teeth were glowing white, and the rest of her, as she came down the steps, was a shapeless, dark blob.

"Hein, hein, hein!" cried this apparition. *"Mes amis!"*

"Marie, *nous sommes arrivés."* said Maricot. *"Et je t'ai apporté un p'tit cadeau—j'espère que tu l'aimeras."*

The woman broke into the most raucous laugh Dorothy had ever heard. Her voice was raspy anyway, and when she laughed it really creaked and croaked. *"Hein, hein, hein,"* she coughed. *"Un cadeau, un bijou, si?"* Maricot gave the woman something. But Dorothy couldn't see what the gift was, but apparently the woman liked it.

"Ah, la, la," she chortled, *"ça me donnera l'air d'un jeune warraron de vingt ans!"* She gave a whoop of joy, and as she moved into the range of the headlights, Dorothy could see the woman's face was lined with twin scars running down each cheek like tiny ski tracks.

"Et où est la p'tite?" Maricot took the woman's arm and guided her toward the wagon, where Dorothy still clung to the last vestige of familiarity. She was astounded that her mother seemed to know this bizarre creature. Who was she?

Raoul was taking the groceries inside the house like it was just ordinary suppertime. Dorothy goggled as she saw the woman approach in the headlights.

She had a very complex face—Dorothy understood this at once. She was getting to know how to judge people's faces. The Fat Man at the deli, for instance. His face was just one thing, one idea—he wanted to take home as much money as he could get, and that was what was in his face —get the money. Marvin Berman, at school, he was just one thing too—like a fox or a weasel, he'd lie in wait to catch you at something, and when he did then he could tease you about it, or get some of it, if it was a Mounds bar or something. That was Marvin's one thing—on the lookout.

But this woman. Wow! In the ten or twelve steps she took to reach the wagon, Dorothy saw a dozen different attitudes and emotions flicker in and out of her eyes: she could see (1), that this woman deferred to Maricot, but at the same time (2), was bent on impressing her. Also, (3), that while she tried hard to give a gay and carefree impression, there was (4), something sinister and not at all jolly about the thick smile drawn back over the slippery white teeth. And what about that horrendous laugh—was that for real?

The woman stood grinning by the open door on the passenger side. *"Bon soir, ma petite, et comment tu t'appelle, hein?"* Dorothy just stared at her, amazed. The grin got even wider, and Dorothy could see that at least half her teeth were gold!

"Alors, mon t'chou, faut pas tegener." She pushed her

mammoth head inside the cab. *"Mais quel' jolie p'tite, café au lâit, comme maman, exact'ment."* She dropped her voice to a conspiratorial whisper. *"Un, deux, trois années et tu auras une très belle corbeille de noce. Tu lever un lapin, hein? Un beau monsieur de commun, pas un mosquito avec un coeur comme un artichaud, mais un amant constant, un vrai constant le plus fort, le plus beau. Maintenant, comment tu t'appelle?"*

Her French sounded funny, not like Mommy's at all. Dorothy could barely understand it; she caught something about coffee and Mommy and one, two, three years and an artichoke and what was her name.

"Je m'appelle Dodo." This made the woman laugh some more.

"Dodo! *Mais j'ai une bonne amie 's'appeller Zozo, c'est presque la même chose, si, Dodo? Ici, nous avons les Fais-do-do, tu connais les Fais-do-do, Dodo?"* The repetition of the syllables and this weirdo lady saying them like that sounded funny and made Dorothy burst into a giggle despite herself, for she hadn't meant to. At this, the woman grinned so widely Doe thought her face would split, and suddenly, with adderlike quickness, she seized Doe about the waist and lifted her easily from the car. Doe was amazed at how strong she was. Her instinct was to struggle, but she felt that would antagonize the lady, and that was one thing Doe sure didn't want to do. The lady held Doe to her fat breasts and brought her face up close to hers.

" 'Suis Marie Laveau, Dodo, *répétez après moi:* Marie Laveau." She waited expectantly, and Dorothy realized she wasn't going to be released until she had repeated the name.

"Marie Laveau," she said, obediently.

"Très bien, petite, très bien. Hokay, Dodo, *tu aime le tac-tac, si?"*

"Oui," said Dorothy, having no idea what tac-tac was, but moving toward the house because she saw Madame Laveau reach for her hand. She didn't like people touching her unless she knew them very well, but there didn't seem to be anything to do about this. She let Madame Laveau take her inside.

The downstairs of the house had an overstuffed couch and a massive teakwood dining table. Lining the mantelpiece was a row of little red clay jars, and there were coals burning in the fireplace, making it uncomfortably warm.

Tac-tac turned out to be, of all things, popcorn. The idea didn't fit the big black woman at all, but Dorothy knew now that nothing Marie Laveau did would be a surprise. She was obviously capable of flying to the moon on a bullrush if she wanted to.

"Hokay, Dodo, *ma Fais-do-do, si tu habite ici avec moi dans le Bayou, tu auras bientôt les pieds d'un canard, hein?"* In illustration, Madame Laveau gave a pair of quacks and waddled grotesquely across the room.

This was getting like *Alice in Wonderland,* Dorothy thought. First they kidnap me, then they bring me to a swamp, and now I have to speak French with Aunt Jemima. *"Madame Laveau, s'il vous plait, parle anglais,"* she said.

Maricot's voice came from the kitchen. *"Non, non, Dorothy, continuer en français. Tu as l'accent très distingué, pense-tu, Marie?"*

"Si, si, d'accord. Alors, Dodo, *ma Fais-do-do."* (She was apparently tagged with this nickname for the duration.) *"Des tac-tac, hein? Manger, manger."* In her thick black hand she offered Dorothy an aluminum foil baking pan filled with popcorn.

"Pas avant le diner," Maricot called in. From the kitchen came the sound of sizzling meat, the smell of frying hamburger.

Madame Laveau nodded her head eagerly, grinning conspiratorially. *"Allez, allez,"* she insisted, and Doe was so hungry she grabbed a fistful of it and stuffed it into her mouth. Marie Laveau rocked back on her giant haunches, beaming, as Maricot came from the kitchen with a tray of four (mismatched) glasses and set Deer Park water and milk on opposite sides of the big Spanish-looking table.

"Why can't I have Coke?" Doe whined.

Maricot smiled tolerantly. *"Parce-que le lait ne contien pas les cyclamates, mon ange."*

"I want a Coke." Maybe I have to obey them in the big things, Doe thought, but I can still make my own kind of trouble at the dinner table. She saw her mother cast her a thoughtful glance.

"Peut-être si tu demande en français, avec la politesse, Dorothy."

Doe sighed. *"Chére maman, belle maman, gentille maman, donnez-moi un* Coca-Cola, silver plate."

At the head of the table, Marie Laveau gave a loud chortle. Maricot shook her head silently and marched back into the kitchen with that sigh of resignation common to all parents whose children have complied with the letter of the law but not the spirit.

From somewhere outside Dorothy thought she heard the sound of male laughter, and then a screen door slammed shut in the rear of the house. A moment later Raoul appeared.

"We eating?" he inquired, and Dorothy was glad to see him because she knew he couldn't speak French.

Maricot came back from the kitchen with a plate of raw vegetables which she set before Raoul, and a glass of Coca-Cola which she gave Dorothy. With a smile of triumph, Doe immediately took a long, three-gulp swallow.

"I don't like her drinking that shit," said Raoul.

"She was a good girl, lahv. She's been speaking French."

"Oh, right," said Raoul, in a mocking tone, "that'll make her much healthier."

"Raoul, darling, I do lahv you dearly, but you've got to stop being such a health nut. You're positively a physique freak. There's more to a person than just the body, you know."

"L'esprit, l'esprit!" cried Marie Laveau, and as she spoke, Doe saw her face puff out like a balloon, enlarging in size until it was equal to the mass of her body, she looked like a float in the Macy's Thanksgiving Day Parade, the Marie Laveau float, and at the same time Doe felt herself rise from her chair until she seemed to float above the table except she knew she was still sitting at the same level as everybody but she was floating on top at the same time and suddenly she knew they had given her the shitty stuff again, it was in the Coke, and the really funny thing was she had *asked* for it, she had made Mommy take back a glass of perfectly good milk and bring back the shitty stuff. This struck her so funny that she broke into laughter, he he, he he, he he, little, short, double-syllabled bursts of laughter and now they were looking at her, Mommy and the retard and Madame Laveau, they were studying her intently, and Madame

Laveau's head was shrinking back to its normal size, and even smaller, like those pinheads she saw at the freak show that time with Frankie—Madame Laveau was a pinhead! And this made her laugh even harder, the tiny head on top of that massive body. Oh, this is hysterical, he he, he he, he he, and then she saw pinhead Laveau get up from the table and come to her and extend her hand and and say "*tiens*" and Doe took the outstretched outsized hand. It was like a boxing glove, it was like a giant chili bean baked onto the end of her arm by mistake, he he, he he, he he, and then they were moving through the house through the kitchen and she couldn't stop laughing, it was all so funny, and out the screen door at the back (that must be where Raoul came from), and into the back yard where oh, oh, oh, look at all the black people. Hey, there's a chicken coop—a *chicken coop?*—with a real chicken in it and in a funny wooden collar thing, across the yard was a goat, a black goat. Oh, goody, we're going to the zoo he he, he he, he he, I haven't been to the zoo since I was a kid, just a kid. Of course now I'm not a kid anymore—I'm a glass of milk, he he, he he, he he, and she's putting me down on . . . What is this, a bed, a boat, a boot, a beet, a bite. This is a really weird zoo. Now why would anybody bring a glass of milk to the zoo?

15

There were six round black firepots placed in a circle about the yard. They cast flickering shadows on the Société—the twenty-five or more people, ranging from high yaller to dark chocolate—Cajuns, Creoles, and an occasional Spaniard—who had come to take part in the ceremony.

They were circling Dorothy's pallet slowly, moving counterclockwise to the rhythm of their chant: *"Marie-Cocotte, li grande zombie! Marie-Cocotte, li grande zombie!"*

In the center, under a canopy constructed from an army surplus tarpaulin, Doe lay on her back on the platform where Marie Laveau had placed her. She was still giggling, he he, he he, and bicycling her arms in the air, as if she were doing the Australian crawl.

The kid is in cuckooland, thought Raoul, as he came out the screen door, carrying the assator. He brought the drum under the tarpaulin and placed it to the left of the platform. He pushed a pang of pity from his mind. He had worked hard to inure himself against any feeling for the kid, because of what they were going to do to her. Don't make friends in the army, he remembered. Even now he

her, to fire her with a malevolent spirit, to make a killer of her.

Below the cross Maricot drew the tomb, the sarcophagus. She decorated it gaily with dots and squiggly lines and lightning-bolt designs and two sceptres emanating from each end.

Maricot stepped back from the vever and sifted the remaining flour in a circle perhaps twelve feet in diameter. She set the bucket aside and approached Raoul.

"Gahsoline," she said, and Raoul could hear the scratchiness in her voice, could see the perspiration standing out on her burnt sienna flesh. She had stuck the chacha handle into her waist. It bounced at her belly like some obscene tumor. somehow he could not break the rhythm, couldn't take his hands from the drum. He gestured with his head to the can on the ground.

"All right," she barked hoarsely. "I'll do it." She picked up the heavy can with the long spout, and though it was not easy to manage, Maricot poured out a perfect circle of high-test, dousing the flour with which she had surrounded the *vever*. She put the can down and moved to the inner edge of the Société.

The men and women had not stopped chanting, but they were passing around a quart bottle of Budweiser that had been refllled, Maricot could smell, with *tafia*, the rummish liquor much like the clairin she knew from Haiti. They were a coarse, adulterated lot, Maricot could see now, and she didn't like them, these Creoles down here. They were treating this as a sideshow, a circus, they weren't serious, they were just getting off on it. Voodoo Saturday Night. She suddenly resented Marie Laveau's lack of taste in collecting such a motley mélange, and she straightened her back regally. I'll show them, with their sly, cynical eyes, their opportunism. I'll show them, she thought.

"Matches," she said to the circle. "Who has matches for me?"

The littlest man, the one they called Rabougri, had some kind of black, gnarled cheroot in his mouth. With a grin that bordered on the lascivious, he took the thing from his lips and extended it toward Maricot.

"Matches," she stated with deadly calm. *"Pas cigarettes, allumettes."* She stuck out her hand impatiently.

There was a murmur of discontent around the circle,

surly eyes peering blackly out from beneath kerchiefs and stockings. Then Rabougri, who seemed more intelligent than the others, reached into his dirty chino pants and drew out an old Zippo lighter. With a slight, but nonetheless mocking, twirl of the wrist, he handed it to Maricot.

Wordlessly she turned and made her way to where she had painted the flour with gasoline. Flipping open the lighter, she flicked the flint into flame and tossed it contemptuously aside.

There was an instant eruption, and like light flooding into a neon sign, the ring of flour was ablaze in less then ten seconds.

Dear Ghêde, she thought, dear Baron Samedi, she whispered, for voicing aloud had become unimportant, this was private now. Let me show you the totality of my devotion, the strength of my obeisance. Let me show you what I can withstand for you.

And in her bare feet Maricot began to dance in the flaming gasoline.

Around the compound, the Société ceased its murmuring, as Maricot placed first toe, then heel, before her, following the ring around with dexterous, graceful little dancer's steps, bringing her knees no higher than a few inches from the ground. It was almost like tightrope walking, balancing on the wet chain of burning flour.

Within Raoul something was in motion. He couldn't stop his compulsive drumming, though the crowd was no longer chanting. He could smell the gasoline mingling with the carbon stench of the firepots, and soon, he thought, the odor of seared flesh. She really wants that hundred seventy five grand, he reflected.

Little gasps of breath escaped Maricot's throat with each footfall as she brought her slim feet down again and again on the smoking flour. She was a *canzo* now, a fire initiate; to summon Baron Samedi she had endured the scorching heat of flame. She came full circle to the point she'd started from, and Marie Laveau crossed the earthern floor and gave her the machete. Maricot took it in her right hand and placed the blade, cutting edge in, within the joint of her left arm, and Raoul saw her bringing her fist to her shoulder, squeezing the soft flesh into the sharp steel. Involuntarily, he winced at the agony Maricot was feeling.

Except she wasn't.

She had brought her fist to within three inches of her shoulder, Raoul had seen her biceps rise beneath her skin and bend before the gleaming edge of the blade, yet when she relaxed her arm there was no incision, and no blood. Impossible, he told himself, and yet—she'd done it. He was seized with a sudden urge to examine the machete, as if he were the victim of a cleverly plotted magician's trick. Yet what Maricot did now was even more amazing.

Placing the point of the blade at her navel she grasped the machete's handle firmly in both hands, shut her eyes, and slowly began pushing the knife into her belly. This is hara-kiri, Raoul thought. He saw the firm belly muscles depress beneath the pressure of the machete's point. He saw the slim layers of skin enfold the tip of the blade, he saw it press yet another quarter inch inward. He waited for the bright, cherry explosion of blood to spurt from her. And waited. And waited. Maricot's arms were trembling with the force she was exerting, pushing the knife into her belly, her eyes were closed, her lips were parted. The moment seemed endless.

Baron Samedi, great Ghêde, she was thinking, know that I am serious in my intention. That I do not summon you lightly. That I am prepared to withstand whatever pain I must to bring you to my child. That I stand ready to follow your bidding. That you may try me with wrathful fire, with sharpest steel, with agonizing pain. With insanity. With disease. With fits. I stand ready to follow you, for you are my God. I test myself, you see, I do not wait to be asked to prove my sincerity. I am ready to withstand anything.

Maricot withdrew the machete. She returned it to Marie Laveau. There was an awed rustle, a murmur from the Société. With this demonstration, she had won them. She didn't care anymore. They were beneath contempt.

The flaming gasoline had diminished to a few fitful pockets, and these would go out momentarily. Marie Laveau took a small cake of some kind—it looked like corn—and, crossing the charred circle of flour, placed it on the lower line of the *vever* Maricot had drawn, the line defining the sarcophagus's bottom.

Inside the mesh chicken coop were six chickens, most of them sleeping now, a couple emitting petulant squawks now and then. Marie Laveau lifted the top of the coop, reached in, and selected the plumpest, healthiest bird of the lot.

Not perfect, thought Maricot, as Marie Laveau handed her the fowl. I hope this chicken will please Baron Samedi; it could use another week's feeding.

The next part of the ritual called for a cleansing and purification of the onlookers. Maricot turned toward the Société. She was half-tempted to forgo this. Baron Samedi, she intoned mentally, these people are not worthy, they are scum, disbelievers, they are lice, vermin, worse than tics, worse than slugs, worse than leeches—but something stopped her. Something unknown, indefinable, a *force majeur,* a power beyond the earthen yard, beyond the house, beyond the parish, beyond the world. No, it spoke to her, these are my people, all of them. Someday they will join me in the other world, *le grand bois d'ilet,* the Island Below the Sea, as you will. It is an act of arrogance to think thus of them. Do not exclude them.

So Maricot secured the chicken by its neck and legs and passed it over the head and shoulders of each member of the Société, now bending in awe before her. And as the men lifted their hats, and the women their kerchiefs, their sins and uncleanlinesses were drained from them and gathered into the pullet; and then the force commanded her to lift and swing the bird over her head by its feet, around in a circle, to air it, to *ventailler,* to rid the beast centrifugally of all these impurities.

And now the bird must face one more trial, the consumption of the corncake. If in its confused and dizzied state the animal could eat the cake, this would be a sign that Baron Samedi was ready to accept the first sacrifice. Maricot brought the bird within the frame of the peristyle, to the bottom leg of the sarcophagus. Gently she ran her hand to the back of the chicken's head, and guided the yellow beak to the cake.

There was a moment's pause, as the chicken oriented itself; then, slowly, but with increasing appetite, the bird began pecking at the cake. Maricot smiled. This was a good sign. She slid her hand under the bird's belly, lifted it, and cradled it in her arms like a baby. She ran her right hand over the chicken's head and bent its neck down in a painful semicircle. Then, choosing her spot with deliberation, she bent her head to the back of the fowl's neck and sank her firm, even teeth into the grayish white feathers. She bit down with all her force. There was the ripping sound of torn cartilage and the pullet gave a convulsive shake, but Maricot held it firmly, opened her jaws, and bit again, twisting her head from side to side until a bite-size piece of flesh was torn from the chicken's neck. Strangely, there was no blood; only a pitiful caw from the mutiated animal's beak.

Maricot spat the piece of neck to the ground and brought the bird once again to her jaws. This time, as her teeth came away from its neck, her mouth was a bright red stain, and a gout of blood leaped nearly a foot in the air; she had cut an artery, and the bird's wings were beating wildly, flapping at its captor's hip and breast, but there was no escape. Maricot spat chicken neck to the ground, and with one final chomp severed the bird's head from its body. She hurled the head from her, and with both hands tried to contain in her grasp the wildly fluttering carcass that spouted dark liquid globules from its neck.

Marie Laveau was right there. As Maricot turned the bird upside down, she held a coffee can beneath the torn neck, catching the blood as it flowed. I must anoint Dorothy, Maricot was thinking, it's time for the *laver-tête,* I must anoint her with the blood of this sacrifice, I must wash her head, for it will act as the vessel of possession, and must be free from all impurity. I must cleanse Dorothy.

She stood above her child, looking down from eyes burning with a glittering, almost messianic purpose. Her mouth was a smear of red, and perspiration hung on her forehead. Dipping two long, tapered fingers into the coffee can, Maricot painted two streaks of blood across Dorothy's forehead. Then, with a single finger, she painted three cross strokes, vertical against the other lines. Dorothy moaned softly and turned over on her back. Maricot bent and kissed her lightly on both eyes, leaving traces of blood on the lashes.

Marie Laveau had brought the goat to the edge of the peristyle. At this distance, Raoul could see that blue velvet ribbons decorated the goat's horns. He was reminded of the piñatas he had seen in Mexico—That's what the goat looked like, a toy piñata, and now Maricot was behind the goat, reaching underneath the animal, reaching for something and reaching again, moving her hand back and forth in a steady rhythm. What the hell was she doing? And the goat gave three rapid steps. Something was disturbing it. The goat shifted position by about ten inches, and now Raoul could see what Maricot was doing—she was moving her fingers gently and sensually over the goat's testicles. Raoul knew what that felt like, and now he could see the small, eager bud of the goats cock, peeking pink from inside its foreskin as it became aroused, and Maricot took the foreskin in her other hand, pulling it up and down over the goat's penis, and up again and down, and the animal's eyes were getting wilder, as Maricot increased the rhythm, and Marie Laveau was steadying the goat, holding it in place as it became more and more excited and Maricot went faster and the goat's cock was long now, and pink, and slick with wetness, and Maricot drew her hand to her mouth and licked her fingers, and encircled the goat's penis again, taking it between the circle of her thumb and forefinger, sending the elongated, rigid goat's cock into a final spasm, and then holding, holding, as the beast lowered its head and crumbled into its own release, bent to its foreknees, but remaining upright on its hind legs, and Maricot didn't take her hand away, she milked the last drop into her palm, as she cooed to the goat, almost like a lover, her eyes half closed, seemingly in a state of trance, and she rose to her feet, careful not to lose any of the liquid in her cupped palm. And the words ran through her head: Oh, Ghêde, Baron Samedi, here is the seed of your symbol, the goat, *Dogwé,* the satyr, phallic, the symbol of your eternal masculine power, your primal hold on us all, through these seeds shall you visit my child, your devotee—through these seeds, through this kiss—And Raoul was transfixed by the sight of Maricot bringing her cupped hand to her mouth, taking the goat sperm on her tongue, and diving animalistically on Dorothy, kissing her, opening her lips with her tongue, sharing the fruit of the goat's orgasm with her daughter. Holy shit! Raoul thought, and had to bend beside the drum and retch upon the dark, chocolaty earth.

Yet his palms did not leave the assator. His hands were magnetized to it.

Dorothy's eyes fluttered rapidly as Maricot tongued the sticky substance into her throat, urging her. Drink, drink, my angel, and in this way shall Baron Samedi visit you, and she reached behind her for the coffee can, which now contained, in addition to chicken blood, the goats testicles as well. She emptied the contents of the can over the lines of the *vever,* retracing in blood and flesh what she had drawn in flour. It was her duty to feed the loa, to propititate the God Ghêde, and so she was giving him blood from a freshly killed chicken and the manhood of a black goat by way of nourishment.

Then, taking the machete, she killed the goat, with four short strokes to the neck. As the machete came down for the fourth time, as Marie Laveau's strong black arms held the horns, as the blood poured over her naked feet, Maricot prayed yet again to the loa: Oh Ghêde, Lord of the Dead, Baron Samedi, please . . . come to my child . . . mount her . . . possess her . . . infuse her spirit.

The goat's body slumped to the ground before the peristyle, the blood seeping from its neck in an ever widening circle.

Marie Laveau helped Maricot wipe the mixed blood and perspiration from her face, hands, and feet with a damp bath towel. Maricot sat on the back steps of the house like a fighter between rounds. She looked out at the circle of Cajuns and Creoles contemptuously.

The Société had fallen silent. Now they were disapproving. When they realized that Maricot meant to possess a child they had withdrawn their sympathy. Children were not equipped, not prepared for a relationship with a loa, and especially not *this* loa. When they heard Maricot call upon Baron Samedi, they began actively to resent her. If Baron Samedi were indeed to mount the child, he could harm her, overwhelm her, she might not be able to deal with him, she might not endure him. Maricot spat on the ground.

Marie Laveau was reading her thoughts. She waved a derisive hand at the circle. "*Les Bajoes,*" she said, and it was true. They were *bajoes,* pigfaces, illiterates. They were not worthy to serve. Next time Marie would choose more carefully.

"Maricot, come here." It was Raoul. Something was happening within the peristyle, under the tarpaulin. A low murmur, coming from Dorothy. Maricot walked quickly to the platform.

" . . . *est mon tabac . . . mon tabac . . .* " Dorothy was

moaning, turning her face from left to right. " . . . *mon tabac, où est mon tabac* . . . " and they both noticed Dorothy's voice had dropped about a fifth, to a much lower pitch, a deeper timbre . . . and now she rose to her knees on the mattress, her hands making short, almost comic gestures of impatience. The eyes flew open.

"Où est mon tabac?" she shouted, and as Maricot stared at her daughter, she knew her invocation had been answered. Baron Samedi was never without his tobacco; if he didn't have a cigar or cigarette, he could be easily antagonized.

"Cigarettes," she said to Raoul, and then remembered he didn't smoke. She rushed to the Société, searched out Rabougri.

"Tabac, Rabougri, immédiatement!" The Société was clearly hostile. They drew back a step. The little man spread his hands in a gesture that indicated he had no tobacco.

"Ne me dites pas un menterie!" she said, furiously bringing her face close to his. Cowed, he reached instantly into the back pocket of his soiled chinos and came up with a gnarled cheroot. Maricot snatched it, brought it quickly back to the peristyle. She saw Raoul staring cautiously at Dorothy.

"She's speakin' Creole," he whispered.

Maricot handed Dorothy the cheroot. The child took it, held it away from her face with amused suspicion. She placed it to her ear and rolled it between her thumb and fingers, listening for the dry crackle of the leaves. When none was forthcoming, she ran the misshapen thing twice beneath her nose, sniffing deeply. She made a wrinkled face, then shrugged. *"Cheval donné, on ne regarde pas à la bride,"* she said, and winked. She hopped off the platform to the ground, put her fists on her hips, and strutted once around the vever like a little dictator. She was acting like Mussolini. She tilted her chin to Raoul at a belligerent angle. *"Du feu?"* she enquired. Maricot picked up the Zippo.

"Non, bomose!" the little figure shouted at Maricot. She pointed an imperious finger at Raoul. *"C'est un p'tit homme, mais il a le coeur bien placé."* She wanted Raoul to light her cigar. Raoul looked at Maricot, and she tossed him the Zippo. He flicked the wheel and held the lighter for Dorothy. As the child puffed strenuously at the che-

root, filling the air with a cloud of foul-smelling smoke, her eyes were fixed on Raoul, mischievously.

Now she spoke one sentence in English, and as she did, her voice dropped another octave—thickened and coarsened until it sounded like something from the jungle, something with blood on its lips. The change in tone was so shocking to Raoul that he almost didn't hear the sense of what the creature (it was hard to think of her as Dorothy) said. What she said was: "You know, once I go in . . . I don't come out."

Something unearthly had spoken. They all heard it, and Marie Laveau, who had joined them under the tarpaulin, gave a short grunt of terror. Raoul was very frightened, and he thought again of making Maricot reverse whatever process she had set in motion. He looked at her, and her hand was clutched to her mouth, hearing Dorothy speak in this voice. He was about to speak when he saw the goat's carcass, the goat that had been slain not twenty minutes before, begin to heave, to puff up and down, in and out. With no one near it or touching it, it seemed to fill with air and then deplete, as if at the mercy of some giant bellows.

And it was happening to Dorothy too—her belly was pumping up and down. One moment she looked pregnant, the next she was a famine victim, as if huge amounts of air were being forced down her throat and then squeezed out of her. And it was the strangest thing—she was recognizably herself again, and her little gasps were in her own voice once more.

Maricot knew what was happening: *cambé.* Dorothy had been seized by Baron Samedi in anger, the spirit had been somehow offended; Maricot did a quick recap of the ceremony: I have cleansed myself, she remembered, I have made invocation, I have drawn the vever, shown the gravity of my intention with the machete and the burning gasoline, I have offered a chicken and a goat as sacrifice, I have opened the road to possession with the kiss of goat seed—where am I in error? The chicken, it must be the chicken.

If she had to she would start the whole thing over again, send for fresh animals, bathe again, everything, yes, tonight, we cannot afford to waste one precious day, Dorothy must receive the Lord of the Dead *now,* before Dusty changed the policy.

She heard Dorothy say something, and turned to see her standing above the heaving goat carcass.

"Prikratee eta duratskoye povyedyena" (Stop this idiotic behavior), "a to, ya tebya pashlyu k chyort ovoy matevi" (or I will see your soul rot in hell forever.)

It was Russian, Maricot realized, and then, with a thrilling shudder, she knew Baron Samedi had mounted Dorothy, for she was speaking in tongues. As a child, in Haiti, Maricot had heard those who had been mounted speak in languages of which they had no knowledge. It was a sure sign.

The carcass of the dead goat subsided obediently, apparently in response to Dorothy's command. When it was quite still, Dorothy bent from the waist, seized the goat beneath the neck and shanks, and, using not her legs but her belly muscles, straightened up, raising the goat high above her head.

God, thought Raoul, that's an eighty-five-pound press, and Maricot smiled with satisfaction. She had also seen people, when mounted, perform feats of impossible strength.

Dorothy began strutting about the compound, carrying the dead goat like a victorious hunter, home with the kill. She approached the inner ring of the Société, and some shrank back in fear, but some remained, awed and fascinated by this tiny warrior, this insolent, strutting child who seemed at once to be someone different, an authority, someone who held answers to mysteries.

Dorothy stopped and surveyed them with a gaze both contemptuous and inviting, almost a smirk. When she spoke, her voice was back in that terrifying bass register, cold and mocking.

"Qui veut à danser?"

Nobody moved. Dorothy stood, her feet pressing their shape into the earth from the added weight of the goat she held above her. *"Alors,"* she repeated, *"qui veut à danser avec moi?"* She shifted her hold beneath the goat, drew the carcass back over her head, and with tremendous force catapulted the goat's body twenty feet over the heads of the Société.

There was a gasp of shock from everyone. No ten-year-old girl could have done this. Dorothy stretched out her bloodied hands. "Rabougri!" she cried, seizing him by the wrist, and flinging him to the center of the compound.

The little man was horror-stricken. Was he going to lose his life at the hands of this tiny demon? Was he going to be mounted by a loa?

"*La musique!*" Dorothy yelled, in her deep tones. "'*La Banda*'!" and the call galvanized Raoul at the assator. He began drumming furiously as Dorothy strutted around the frozen Rabougri in her insolent, military strut. She circled him twice, letting the rhythm take effect, seep into her, and then began to beckon him lewdly, suggestively, rolling her pelvis from side to side.

After a few moments, Rabougri sensed he was not going to be harmed. He joined her, and the pair danced together around the peristyle. Dorothy made open advances to Rabougri, often sliding her hands over his flanks and crotch, but Rabougri was too intimidated to respond. He kept a cautious distance between them.

On the steps, Maricot smiled grimly. Baron Samedi was here, all right, in her child. Calling for "La Banda" had been the final proof, if she needed any, after seeing that goat fly into the brush. "La Banda" was Ghêde's dance, gay and suggestive. Ghêde was often mischievous, as with the cigar and the lighter, then, mercurially, he could turn suddenly harsh, demanding, and deadly. There was no controlling him, You were at his mercy, and he could invest you with unbelievable powers or force you to obey his darkest impulses. Once mounted, you were at the mercy of your loa, whether kind or evil depending on how well you had propitiated the spirit.

Dorothy danced for an hour and forty minutes straight. Several times Rabougri tried to beg off, to leave, for he was exhausted. But Dorothy would not let him go, kept plucking him back into the circle around the vever.

They had danced all over the drawing, by now the flour and gasoline, the blood and the goat's testicles had been mashed into a dark, pinkish mass.

Finally, Rabougri sat down on the ground, right in the middle of the vever, and with helpless, breathless gestures indicated he could not go on. Maricot was afraid that Baron Samedi would punish him for this defection, but Dorothy, never stopping her dance, merely booted him off in a friendly fashion, back to the Société, and continued dancing by herself.

She danced another hour and ten minutes. It was nearly two thirty in the morning, yet she was dancing faster now. It was hard to believe. Raoul had finally abandoned the drum, his hands had given out. And still Dorothy danced, without any rhythm but the one inside her head, increasing her tempo, raising her knees higher, bringing her soles down harder on the firm black earth, her breath a harsh rasp within her throat.

Maricot began to fear for Dorothy. Her body wasn't hers anymore—it was merely an instrument, mounted by Baron Samedi and forced to his will. He could kill Dorothy if he chose to, could turn this into a dance of death, if he were angered or dissatisfied. Twice Maricot thought she saw Dorothy peering out in anguish from pained eyes. It was a strange concept—the body did not belong to its owner, it belonged to its possessor, and while he was inside, he could do with it what he might.

Finally, Ghêde released her, and she dropped as if shot to the earth. Maricot and Raoul rushed to her. The girl lay panting on the ground. As each hoarse breath tore from her throat, Dorothy sprayed tiny gouts of blood-flecked saliva. There was fear in her eyes, the kind of fear you see in old men lying in the street, waiting for the ambulance, in those who know they are about to die and are fighting it with every breath. Dorothy was afraid of this. Maricot wondered if this were the price Ghêde was going to exact eventually.

As she and Raoul carried Dorothy into the house, Maricot prayed Baron Samedi would ask a little less of Dorothy tomorrow night.

16

Dusty kept the Pinto at an even sixty-five, all the way down Route 10. He drove nearly an hour and forty minutes before he was able to leave the big highway for 167, and he knew he only had a few more miles to go until he got to Pinhook Road. He rubbed his eyes, wondering if he could talk the Sheraton Town House into letting him take a shower in one of their bathrooms. He felt sticky and unshaven; he'd been up all night.

The flight had stopped in Atlanta, had finally spit him off in New Orleans at seven fifteen this morning. What a goddamned milkrun. If he'd known Lafayette was actually closer to Baton Rouge, he could have flown in there. Ah, what the hell, Paul Cobb was paying. He had been so nervous, afraid some flight clerk would catch a discrepancy in the signature he'd practiced twenty-two times in the men's room at Kennedy, and it would be all over. No one had even looked. Not at Delta, not at Hertz, and probably not at the Sheraton Town House either, if he checked in and took a shower.

The highway ran over swampy marshland, and the humidity was stifling. He turned his gaze to the sky, bleak gray, overcast. It had been threatening to rain for the past three days, Dusty had learned in New Orleans; each day the forecast had been for heavy squalls, but "God was jes' foolin' with us, Mr. Cobb," the girl at Hertz had murmured, in her soft Southern accent, while filling out his form, "jes' foolin' around."

Pinhook Road loomed up on the right, and he made the turn. Christ, look at it, he thought. Shopping malls and Texaco stations and a Pancake House—it looks like New Jersey, it looks like the whole fuckin' country, this is how it is everywhere. The stifling ordinariness, the sudden familiarity hitting him in a place he'd never been, hitting him with the universal and acceptable mediocrity that is most of the USA, suddenly depressed him. He was glad the sun wasn't out—in this heat it would be unbearable.

And there was the Sheraton, with a sign advertising the entertainment in the Town Lounge—Tues–Sat: Dini Haskell and The Ladds. He could imagine. Their opening number would be "I Believe in Music."

He drove around to the parking lot in the back of the motel. All the cars in the lot were parked on a diagonal, heads in. Dusty was the kind of guy who liked to back into a parking space. It made getting out much easier.

He went in the back entrance and the first thing that struck him was the Muzak, playing "What a Difference a Day Makes." Better believe it, he thought. The desk was unattended. Dusty leaned over it.

"Hey, anyone minding the store?"

A large man with a thatch of white hair came out of the open office door. "Whah yes, sir. May ah help you?"

Dusty noticed he didn't quite fit in his blue Sheraton jacket, and that he wore a bar on his breast that said MR. FARNON.

"I'm looking for a Mr. Mendoza. I believe he checked in here within the past couple of days. He would've had a little girl with him."

Farnon nodded. "Whah yes, sir, they was here, sure 'nough. But they left yesterday. Are you Mr. Fournier?"

The question caught Dusty off guard. Farnon saw the split second of indecision flash behind Dusty's eyes. " 'Cause ah got a letter here for Mr. Fournier." Farnon smiled. "But ah see you're not the man."

"No, he's a friend of mine," Dusty countered, not wanting to lose the tantalizing glimpse of the trail that had suddenly been revealed to him. "Did Mr. Mendoza say where he was going?"

"No, he surely did not. Just to make sure Mr. Fournier got this envelope. And to ask for an I.D."

"The little girl—did she seem to be . . . is she okay?"

"Now that is one sweet little girl, mah friend. Sweet as corn muffins. How old would that little girl be, can you tell me?"

"She's ten."

"Good Lord above, they sure grow up fast these days, don't they? Ten, Lord above. Yes, she's okay. Wish ah was just as okay as that little girl."

"Ahm, Mr. Fournier told me to meet him here about noon time, said he was picking up the envelope. Is that what you understood, Mister Farnon?"

"Mah friend, ah know nothing of what tahm, what date, or what season Mr. Fournier is expected here. Now that's all ah c'n tell you, ah'm sorry."

" 'Kay, thanks. I'll be back." He went out the front in a frenzy of agitation. He was sure that envelope contained what he needed. How the fuck was he gonna get it? Farnon wanted an I.D. and Dusty's name wasn't Fournier. Fournier, Fournier. He wandered two blocks down Pinhook Road and stopped by a real estate office. He opened the door and stepped inside. There was the jangle of a bell, and a small fortyish lady looked up from her desk.

"Morning, how y'all today?" she said. Jesus they were cheerful down here.

"I'm just fine, ma'am. Would you have a phone directory I could look at for a minute?"

"Ah surely would." She reached into the bottom left drawer of her desk and extracted a volume maybe a half-inch in thickness. "You got the Yellow Pages in there as wayull."

"Thank you." Hurriedly he flipped through to the F's. There were several Fourniers. He selected Phillippe, Haberdasher, on East Vermilion St. and wrote down the number.

From a pay phone in a drugstore, he dialed the store. He had to go through a salesman and a secretary before he was able to speak to Mr. Fournier. He did an impression of Colonel Sanders.

"Mr. Fournier, mah name is Farnon, ah'm at the Sheraton Town House, out on Pinhook. We have a letter here for you."

"I don't know anyone at the Town House."

"Says Fournier Haberdashers raht on the envelope."

"Who's it from?"

"Du'nt say, jes' says Fournier Haberdashers. But holdin' it to the light, ah maght venture to say there's some kahnda check in it."

"A check?"

"Could be."

"Open it up."

"Can't do that, Mr. Fournier, against Sheraton regulations."

There was a pause. "Then I tell you what you do, Mr. Farnon. Write down my address—"

"Now ah'm sorry, Mr. Fournier, we were instructed to deliver this by hand. I'm goin' off at one o'clock. Could you get here sometahm during lunch?"

There was an aggravated sigh on the other end of the line. "All right, I'll send someone."

"Make sure he carries some identification from you, Mr. Fournier—ah can't go givin' checks out to jist anyone."

"Thank you for calling," said Fournier, and hung up.

Dusty ambled back to the Town House. Now all he had to do was watch the desk between now and one this afternoon, and someone from Fournier's would come and claim the letter. From there it would be easy.

He came in the front door this time (the Muzak was playing "I Remember You") and was about to sit down on the couch opposite the Town Lounge when Mr. Farnon spoke to him across the desk.

"Your friend was here," he said. Dusty felt a chill go through him.

"When?"

"Whah, not two minutes ago. Ah told him you'd been in lookin' for him—"

Dusty was on his feet frantically vacillating between the front and rear doors. "Which way'd he go?"

Farnon shrugged unconcernedly. "Maght still catch him in the parking lot."

In the lot a thin mulatto was just climbing into a Chevy Vega.

"Hey, Fournier," Dusty called across the lot, "hold on. I wanna talk to you."

The man sat down in the driver's seat and seemed to huddle protectively into himself. Dusty could tell he was edgy and nervous. He remembered Terri Edison telling him Raoul had done some dealing.

"What's your hurry, Fournier?" Dusty planted himself authoritatively between the man and the open door of the Vega. He saw Fournier's eyes searching craftily for a way out, but the Vega was parked face in and Fournier would have to do a lot of backing and turning before he was in any position to make a getaway.

"I'm looking for Raoul Mendoza, Fournier."

"Connais pas," said Fournier.

"Talk English, pal," Dusty said, doing his Lloyd Nolan impression. It was one of his worst impressions—it always came out too Bogart—but it was working fine on Fournier. "Now where's Mendoza?"

"You are a policeman?"

"Never mind who I am, Fournier," Dusty crackled. "Let's just say I'm interested in the whereabouts of Raoul Mendoza, Caucasian, about five foot ten."

"I don't know where he is, I swear to you, *je le jure."*

"I think you do, Fournier." Dusty let his upper lip slide over his teeth. "I think you have a letter in your pocket right now that tells you just where he is."

"No, I swear."

"Listen, Fournier, you want me to run you in? I could take you downtown and book you on suspicion of being an accessory." He brushed some lint off his sleeve. "But I'm not interested in you, Fournier, you're small potatoes. I want Mendoza. But I'll make it rough for you if I have to, you understand me?"

Fournier was staring at the steering wheel like a kid being lectured. He reached inside his cheap, seersucker jacket and pulled out the envelope. Dusty snatched it, a fierce joy filling his face.

"All right, Fournier, get outta here." Fournier started the motor gratefully. "And don't let me see you round here again."

17

Maricot was furious with Marie Laveau. She had endangered Dorothy's life. The materials and participants she had provided for the ceremony were certainly what had antagonized Baron Samedi. Those *bajoes* and that rotten excuse for a chicken had angered him so that he had whipped Dorothy into the frenzied, three-hour marathon that had left her weak and exhausted, had nearly burst her little heart.

Maricot had been savage with Marie, had spoken angrily and severely to her, and the black woman had cowered under Maricot's lashing and left soon afterward to buy another goat, a fine new chicken, and to recruit fresh members for the Société. An hour ago she had returned and was now out in the compound with Raoul.

There had been a twenty-minute squall about mid-afternoon, and the ground had been muddied. Together, Marie and Raoul were rebuilding the peristyle, which had blown down in the sudden wind. They were tamping the stakes into the earth, making sure the tarpaulin was tented firmly and securely over the platform and the mattress.

She would probably not be able to draw the vever on the ground tonight. Vever called on account of rain, Raoul had joked. So Maricot had painted the cross and the sarcophagus on a large sheet of brown wrapping paper. It would serve.

All day long Maricot had kept Dorothy in bed, had nursed her, feeding her soup and oatmeal, and then, around five thirty, a small steak and some broccoli, to build up her strength. She did not anticipate another ordeal like last night, but Dorothy had to be in shape for whatever was asked of her. She had to become accustomed to being mounted by Baron Samedi. Another three days, maybe four, and Dorothy would be able to conjure him herself. As long as she had the cha-cha.

She glanced at the couch where Dorothy lay inert beneath a blanket, her eyes far away. Maricot knew her spirit had been traumatized by the shock of last night's experience. But Dorothy was a strong child, she would bounce back. Maricot was suddenly overcome by a wave of tenderness for her daughter. She knelt by the couch and took Dorothy's head in her arms, making sure not to scratch the child on her sequin top. She rocked Dorothy gently from side to side.

"Mommy . . . "

"Yes, sweetness, I know. Would you like me to give you some chocolate ice cream?"

"Mommy . . . you're not going to make me . . . do I have to do the dance again tonight?"

"Four more nights, angel, then it's over." And if it's only three, so much the better.

"Four more nights . . . " Dorothy was close to weeping. "Oh, God, I don't think I can do it. . . ." She wasn't sure exactly what it was she couldn't do—all she remembered was dancing until she'd dropped.

"It won't be so bad tonight, sweetness, I promise."

"But Mommy, why am I doing this anyway? What's the point?"

Maricot had the urge to spill it, tell her everything, how they were going to have enough money from Dusty's insurance to do whatever they wanted, she and Doe. She wanted desperately to confide in Dorothy. Of course, it was impossible. She tied her hair back with the blue velvet ribbon.

"Darling," she said softly, "we just have to wait a little while, and then we can be together forever. We'll hahv lots of money, and we'll take lots of trips. Would you like to go back to Disney World? Or Montreal?"

But Dorothy was not to be mollified. "You're not going to make me drink that stuff again, Mommy? Please?"

"No, angel, no more stahff, I promise." Dorothy didn't need the Allocaine anymore, not after the first mounting. It was like sex: after the first time, it was easy—after the resistance was gone.

Dorothy heard Raoul come in the back door, and she froze. A moment later he appeared in the doorway. He gave a short nod.

"Ready for the princess," he said.

Dorothy clutched in fear as Maricot stood up. This was it. She was going to have to go out there again, go through that horrible dance and everything.

"Mommy," she murmured tearfully.

Her mother looked at her with mixed sympathy and determination. "Just make up your mind to it, angel. And keep your eyes and ears open, and you'll learn something." She put out her hand in that no-nonsense way she sometimes did and Dorothy knew there was no way out.

Reluctantly, she rose from the couch and took her mother's hand. Slowly they moved through the kitchen and out onto the steps. The firepots lit pockets of darkness with yellow flame, and she could see the dark ring of the Société waiting for her. She felt the moist breeze on her bare arms and prayed fervently for rain. Maybe if it rained really hard they'd call off the ceremony.

"Here, lahv." Maricot handed her the cha-cha. "You do it tonight. When I point to you, shake it once, but just once, understahnd, sweetness?" Dorothy nodded, and Maricot pointed to her, and she shook the cha-cha, as she had often shaken it, in fun, innocently, over the years. Now the rattle sounded ominous, heavy, like the rattle of dead souls.

"Baron Samedi," her mother was crying. "Hear this child. I call on you to listen to this humble serviteur . . . to receive her, hear her, attend her. . . ."

Dusty pulled the Pinto up behind the Torino wagon and turned it around, face out. The house was still and silent, and because of the wind through the cypresses he could not hear the activity going on in the compound, behind the house. It was really blowing up now; the fat droplets had begun to splatter his windshield about two miles back. He looked at the house cautiously. They're out, he thought. I don't blame them. If I lived here, I'd be out, too.

He walked up the steps, shielding his face in his jacket. When the wind whipped those drops in your face, it could sting, man. He tried the door. It was open. He stepped inside and found himself in a room dimly illuminated by light coming from what must be the kitchen. The couch had a blanket pulled back, as if someone had been napping there. He crossed into the kitchen, and that's when he heard the voices chanting, outside in the back yard. As he made his way to the back door he was listening not only to voices—there was a drum, too—and what they were chanting was nothing he had ever heard before —*fettun vevey poomwah fettun vevey poomwah*—and pushing the screen door out, he found himself on the top step of the back stairs, and there was Dorothy, shaking the cha-cha, and Maricot was dancing in flaming gasoline!

He didn't stop to think. With a giant bound he leaped off the stairs and rushed to Dorothy, scooping her up in his arms. He flashed on the fact that leaping back up the steps to the house would slow him down too much and instinctively headed to his left, around the side of the building, hoping there was at least some little path through the brush. And Dorothy was screaming, Frankie! Frankie! at him as if she couldn't believe it and beating him on the arm with the cha-cha (I knew that cunt had the cha-cha), and he was getting too winded, he had to put her down, but it was better that way, she was faster than he was, and she took him by the hand, leading the way, and together they came out at the front of the house, even as they heard the stunned cries behind them, and as he opened the door of the Pinto, Doe had the presence of mind to jump in lightning fast ahead of him so she wouldn't have to take the time to run around the car and, oh, Christ, the door of the house burst open, and Raoul and Maricot hurtled out like two evil spirits. She had that sequin top on. What the fuck was she doing, Community Theatre down here? And Doe was screaming at him, Frankie, get going, get going, and thank God he'd locked the other door to protect his overnight bag in the back, because there was Maricot, that motherfucker, yanking at the door even as he started the engine and, oh, God, she's coming round the back, and he quick took his right hand off the ignition and jammed the lock down, and a good thing he did because now Maricot was yanking at *his* door putting her hand through the open half of his window reaching for the lock, and he was tempted to rip her fuckin' wrist off, but he started the engine and threw the car in gear even as he heard Raoul revving the Torino behind him and Maricot ran back and jumped in, but the Torino still had to turn around, and the Pinto was facing out!

He could see the Torino's headlights gaining on him in the rearview mirror, streaking, because the rain was coming down heavy now. He knew he should turn on the wipers but there was no way he could take his eyes off the road at this speed—he was doing forty over a dirt road with a bump in the middle and when he reached the junction he ran the STOP sign and zoomed right onto 167, which was a fuckin' ridiculous chance to take, especially in the rain, and when he got to I-90 there would be a four-way light, and he knew he'd have to slow down there, and he could only hope Raoul would run out of gas or have a kidney attack or something, because if Raoul and Maricot were able to stick on his tail all the way to Baton Rouge they could probably get the kid back. Christ, he could barely see the road—

"Dorothy, the wipers! Get the wipers!"

The kid reached over him, the wipers were on the left and first she pulled, and then pushed, and the lights went off, and for a horrible moment the car was in limbo with no wipers and no lights, a hurtling ball of motion in space and then the kid got the lights back on and Dusty saw the road come halfway clear through the windshield as the rubber blade squeegeed the water away, and the Torino was only three lengths in back of him now. Funny they were both Ford cars, the Pinto and the Torino—the Pinto had the advantage on the dirt road, lighter and more maneuverable, but here on the macadam the Torino had the weight and probably the speed . . . Jesus Christ, he's getting closer.

"Frankie! Here he comes! Here he comes!"

"Shut up, shut up I know! I know!"

WRAAAANNNKKK!!!!! there was a terrible jolt as the Torino shot into the Pinto from behind Christ he must be doing ninety I'm doing over eighty and *WWRRRR-AAAAAANNNK!!!!!* the sonofabitch did it again, and Dusty thought, Whiplash, whiplash, and then out of nowhere the world lit up around them with a ghostly grayish, blindingly intense light followed instantly by the loudest crack of thunder Dusty had ever heard and Doe was screaming in terror.

"Frankie! Frankie! It's on top of us!"

Shit, there's the intersection, there's I-90 and it's turning yellow and I see traffic up there and what am I gonna do? He's right behind me. If I slow down he'll get me. Will I have to run this light? Look, it's on the last beat of the yellow it's coming up and, oh, shit, on the right on the right. . . .

"Frankeeeeee watch out—!!!"

He swerved at eighty miles per hour to his left through the light and the guy on his right came up short with a terrible squeal of rubber and Dusty saw him fade into a skid behind him, the poor bastard, but hold on, keep swinging left, keep swinging left, hold the wheel steady, and—

"Aaaaannnhhh, haaaaah haaaaaaannnhhhh. . . . "

Yes, I know, baby, oh, baby, Doe, darling, maybe the poor bastard caught Raoul, wouldn't that be just wonderful? I see lights behind me but maybe it isn't him anymore. Now at least I'm on the Interstate with a passing lane, except don't forget it's two-way traffic, slow down, slow down, you're doing eighty, that passing lane goes both ways—

"Dorothy, are you all right?! Answer me!"

She was hanging over the back seat looking fearfully out the rear window. "Frankie! He's back, he's BACK!!"

The Torino was back, gaining on him. How did he get through that light, the cocksucker, and there was the lightning again and that incredible cannoncrack of thunder as if the world was splitting. God doesn't want me to make it, the bastard, well, fuck you, God, pour it on, I'm making it y' prick and, shit, here he comes again—

"Fraaaaankieeeeeee!!!!"

WWWRRAAANNNNKKKK!!!!! Raoul hit him again and now he fell back a length or so and Dusty saw the headlights in his rearview draw out slightly to the left, behind him, into the passing lane, and then start coming up faster than Dusty thought possible. Jesus, the guy must be doing ninety-five, and suddenly the Torino was abreast of him in the passing lane. He glanced once quickly to his left and he could actually see Maricot through the rain, and the wipers were up to full speed, and he jammed the accelerator to the floor, but the Pinto was giving it everything, it just wouldn't go any faster, and then the Torino cut in to the right. They were trying to force him off the highway, and he was holding the wheel with both hands. Keep tight, keep tight—

"Ohhhhhh nnnooooooo!!!!"

CCCRRRRRAAAAANNNNNNNAAARRRRKKKK!! He felt the Pinto quiver and shake, he heard the whining crunch of tearing steel as the wagon cut into the Pinto's left mudguard. Shit, he's trying to ram my mudguard into my tire, the sonofabitch, here he comes again—*CCCC-CCRRRRAAAAAAANOKKKK OKKKKKK OKKK-KKK!!!! AWWWWWKKKK!!!* God, if he can do that he can immobilize me, and now he could hear the continuing scrape of steel against rubber and the faint beginning smell of burning, and, shit, if he catches me like that once more it's all over and there's nothing I can do. Oh, Christ, here he comes again, no, no, and the kid is screaming, shut up shut up—

Neither of them knew where the big diesel came from but suddenly there it was, its monotone horn blaring hideously in the rainy darkness, its headlights a good five feet above the Torino's and it happened so fast there was no time for anything. The oncoming diesel ploughed into the Torino with the combined impact of a 140 mile-an-hour crash. There was nothing to do. The Torino crumpled, totaled, and burst into flame all in the space of a second, and Dorothy saw the orange glow light the highway even brighter than the lightning, and then she was screaming, screaming, and pounding the seat as through the back window of the Pinto, the cha-cha clutched to her face, she saw her mother incinerated on a highway sixty-two miles from Baton Rouge, Louisiana.

He had to feed her Valium on the flight back. She went in and out of hysteria, sometimes talking quite coherently and then suddenly lapsing into a kind of forced laughter, *he he, he he, he he,* and then breaking down into great, wracking sobs, burying her face in the corner of her seat.

The whole flight was a horror show. They were delayed

forty minutes by a leaking fuel pump, and when they were finally in the air it was nothing but turbulence. The storm lasted up into Virginia and they had to keep their belts on.

He had been apprehensive at Hertz—he was sure by now the alarm was out on Paul Cobb's credit card, and he wasn't up to all that right now—he had the kid to take care of. Amazingly, there was still no trouble, except, of course, the damage to the Pinto. Hit and run, he'd told them, some idiot ran the light, rammed right into me. And they'd taken Paul Cobb's address again, and he'd said, "My insurance company'll take care of it," and they'd said something about partial coverage, and he'd said, "Just let me know," and signed the thing, and oh, Jesus, the orange blaze kept running over and over again on the screen of his mind.

Maricot was dead. He was going to have to deal with that now, himself, he knew, wearily watching Doe drift off into her ten-milligram sleep. And at last the tears came, his tears, delayed until they were finally safe. And he was glad to cry, glad to ventilate the mixture of adoration and hostility he would always hold for Maricot. Oh, Jesus, baby, it was so beautiful with you, you were the best, I feel privileged, I am one lucky sonofabitch to have known you. . . . Why did you have to turn into such a rotten bastard? Why did you have to die?

Doe was groggy and out of it and had to be led into the elevator and upstairs. He had to pull out the Castro. As he slipped the T-shirt over her head he noticed the cha-cha in her right hand and realized she'd been hanging on to it ever since he first saw her in Louisiana hours ago. God, it seemed like ages. Thank God, at least she'd been able to salvage the cha-cha.

"Okay, baby, okay, my little beauty," he crooned to her as he gently tucked her in. "You're home again, my darling, a good night's sleep'll fix you up just fine, and then tomorrow you can tell me all about it, okay? Okay, honey?" He thought he saw the beginning of a smile at the corner of her mouth, and she looked at him as if she understood, but he couldn't be sure. There was something missing in her expression. Let her sleep it off, he thought, as he doused the lamp by the couch. Even as he left the room, Doe was drifting into sleep. And she was clutching the cha-cha in her little hand, as she had always done, ever since she was a baby.

He started awake. His eyes shot open and instantly he knew there was something wrong. Some presence was in the room, something strange and . . . dangerous, he had the insane impression it was some kind of wild animal, and then he heard it. A rattle? Was there a snake in here? And he threw his body around, and that's when he saw her, standing by his bed, and there was something in her face, something he had never seen, and then she made the rattle noise again, and he realized dimly it was only the cha-cha (but it had never sounded like that before).

Jesus, it had really scared him. "Doc?" he said, and she looked at him with that peculiar, dense stare. "Are you all right, honey?"

"I want Mommy," she said simply, and turned and walked away, back into the living room, without another word.

18

"Rossie called," he told her over morning tea. "She said she was hanging your picture up with the others."

"I didn't finish it."

"Yeah, she told me, but she liked it so much she put it up anyway."

She seemed much better this morning—alert, in control of herself, like the old Dodo. It was probably best to see that she swung right back into the routine, Dusty thought, let her get back to normal. "Tonight, after school, I'll tell you about Fat Gina, honey, and you can tell me all about that mumbo jumbo they were doing to you down there, okay?"

"I'll bet Gina cried, didn't she?"

"I'll tell you later, now get going. I promised Rossie you'd be back."

"She's gonna be mad at me for being absent."

"I told her you had to take a trip with Mommy." The minute he said the word "Mommy," he knew he was going to have to monitor his choice of words carefully from now on. The little eyes were filling with tears. It was a mistake to think you could go on acting as if nothing had changed.

The child came to him. She was trying not to weep. He held her. "I know, baby, I know."

"She didn't even have a funeral, Frankie. Not even a little one." She had a cremation, Dusty thought, and it was too good for her.

"I tell you what, darling—we'll hold a service for her somewhere, would you like that?" Doe nodded solemnly. "Where?"

"There's a church I know on Forty-eighth Street, a friend of mine knows the monsignor there. I'll take a ride down this afternoon and talk to him, tell him what happened, how Mommy died, and ask him if he'll arrange some kind of mass." She was crying now, softly and openly, then harder, and he could only hold her and rub her and try to give her some small physical comfort while the drops fell on the kitchen linoleum, and he let her weep for three or four minutes, and when the sobs finally subsided, when they were coming far enough apart, he let her go, and she put on her Disney World sweat shirt (her Ferrari jacket was lost now) and went to the hall.

"You be okay?" he asked her. She nodded wordlessly and shut the door behind her.

All right, he thought. We'll say good-bye properly, give the kid something to hang on to, some ritual she can remember. That's what funerals are for.

Maricot had not embraced any religion. She used to laugh and tell him all she believed in was "mahgic." But he knew the dominant Haitian religion was Catholicism, and a Christian service would do as well as any. Doe had been to synagogue several times, but she was being raised as an atheist. They had both wanted Dorothy to rely on herself, rather than believe in some mystical power, but the Catholic ceremony would be an education. It was time he started teaching her about the different religions of the world.

The only church with which he had any familiarity was the Actors' Chapel on West Forty-eighth Street. He had been there several times with his pals from the Improvisation, usually around Christmas. He had met the monsignor, whose name was Flemyng, and he felt sure if he explained the circumstances, Father Flemyng would accommodate him.

It was two fifteen when Dusty left the Actors' Chapel, walked up to Broadway, and turned downtown. Father

Flemyng had not been available to speak with today, but had sent word for Dusty to come back tomorrow. Dusty thought maybe he'd buy a New Orleans newspaper at the out-of-town newsstand on Forty-third, see if there was any mention of the accident. On Forty-sixth Street he paused by a pay phone and dialed his service. There were three messages: Leonard, Frank Hauser, and the Dalton School. Quickly, he called Dalton and was put through to Mr. Seeger, the assistant principal.

"Mr. Greener, I think you'd better get yourself over here."

"What's wrong, Mr. Seeger?"

Seeger paused, as if thinking it over. "Well, speaking as accurately as I can, Dorothy has defaced an art exhibit."

For once, Dusty was speechless.

"I don't think my daughter would do a thing like that," he said finally.

"It's very puzzling. Dorothy is not an antisocial child. This is the first time she's behaved this way. She simply took a crayon and painted over the other children's pictures."

Dusty checked his watch. It was two twenty-five. "You want me to come get her?"

"I think maybe you should. Normally we'd handle something like this right here, but there's a very disturbing element."

"What do you mean?"

"I want you to see what she drew, Mr. Greener. After that we can talk."

"I'll be there by three," Dusty said.

The Dalton lobby was bare of decoration when Dusty came through the big iron doors. That morning an exhibit of fourth-graders' pictures had festooned the walls, pictures the fourth grade had taken two weeks to complete. Now they had all been taken down.

Mr. Seeger's office was at the end of the hall on the fourth floor, and when Dusty came in he smiled. Seeger was a tall, rangy man with big hands and a face filled with optimism. Dusty had always liked him, ever since they'd met four years before.

Now Seeger indicated the chair by his desk and Dusty

sat down. On the desk were five two-and-a-half-foot-square pieces of art paper, stacked on top of each other. Seeger tamped tobacco into his pipe and nodded at the pile.

"Take a look," he said casually. Dusty leaned forward in his chair and picked one from the pile. The original sketch had been an airplane flying over a house, a common subject in the fourth grade. It was signed "F. Larrabee, Grade 4." There were two trees, one on each side of the house, and the house had two upper windows and a door. The drawing was totally symmetrical. Whoever F. Larrabee was, he or she had an orderly mind.

Slashed across the picture, standing upright, Dorothy had crayoned a massive black cross. The cross's horizontal arm corresponded precisely with the line F. Larrabee had drawn to represent the ground in his picture. Under this line, directly below the vertical leg of the cross, Dorothy had written the initials B.S.

Damn it, Dusty thought. I've got to stop laughing at her when she uses bad language. "This is my fault," he said. "I say things like 'bullshit' in front of her, so she thinks words like that are okay."

"Is that what you think this is?" Seeger asked him.

"I can't think of anything else."

"Look at the next one."

The second picture was the work of Lucy Gross. Lucy was obviously fond of animals. She had drawn a rabbit and a giraffe in cages at the zoo. The rabbit's cage was small, the giraffe's cage was tall, and the giraffe was looking down at the rabbit. A balloon from his mouth had the phrase "Hi, Shorty" in it. Dorothy had painted a black rectangular box over the cages, and on top of the box was another cross. Though there was no articulable reason, he knew instantly the box was a coffin or a tomb. Dusty stared at it for a full minute and a half, until Seeger's voice broke his concentration. "See what I mean?" The teacher picked a pipe off his desk.

"Yes, I do."

"Keep going."

Dusty picked the next drawing off the pile with trepidation. Across Nicole Bernstein's rendition of a sky full of stars, Dorothy had rendered a malevolent black face, a woman's, with twin scars running down each cheek. The face glared from the paper with almost a living presence,

pad. "Okay?" He handed the memo over and Dusty stood up. Seeger came around from behind his desk. "Also, we've warned Dorothy that if anything of this nature occurs again we'll have to suspend her attendance here for an indefinite period."

"Right," said Dusty automatically. He wanted to see his kid. "Where is she?" Seeger glanced at the inside of his wrist.

"They should be about finished with basketball."

As they stepped off the elevator to the gym Dusty heard the echo-ey sounds of shouts reverberating off the walls, and the rubbery sound of basketballs being dribbled.

Dorothy was in the midst of a game. She was a guard, and Dusty noticed her eyes never left the ball as it ricocheted from one player to the next. She was the smallest, the other four—two boys, two girls—were bigger and faster than she was, especially Marvin Berman, a big chunk of a kid who Dusty could tell got his way (when he did) by bullying.

But Doe was quick and agile. Marvin had the ball now, and she kept jumping up into his face, flicking at his eyes with her hand, never quite smacking him but distracting him enough so that he couldn't find an opening to get rid of the ball or shoot it. He tried to pass, feinted left, right, looking for someone in the clear, and finally decided to go with the ball himself. He dribbled once around in a circle, advanced two steps, and poised himself to shoot. At the same moment, Doe threw herself in the air, and as Marvin sprang the ball toward the hoop, tipped it just enough to deflect its arc. Marvin spun away, a look of disgust on his face, and as he did, shot his hip out so it connected with Doe's thigh, sending her sprawling to the ground.

Dusty, watching, was blinded by anger. He had to restrain himself from rushing onto the court and belting the little prick. He looked at Seeger, beside him, and saw the teacher raise his eyes significantly. "I know how you feel," he said. "But remember, that's how Marvin's parents will feel about Dorothy when they see what she did to Marvin's painting."

That piece of shit, Dusty thought. Doe could do it in her sleep. With an effort, he controlled himself.

19

They were sitting in Ralph's, where she loved the spaghetti al pesto. This was a treat for Doe—he had decided not to rebuke her, not to come down on her for the picture incident, until he had heard all about what had happened in Louisiana.

She was telling him everything she could remember: how she had tried to convince the stewardess on the flight down that she was being kidnapped; how they'd held her for two days in the motel with one of them always with her so she couldn't escape; how they'd fed her the shitty stuff—

"Doe, we don't use that word in public. I keep telling you, and I'm not kidding. I've noticed recently your language has gotten really foul, really gross, and I want you to stop it, okay? I'm serious." She looked at him wide-eyed, and his heart went to her. "All right now," he said after a moment. "What stuff did they feed you?"

"I don't know what you call it. You put it in a glass of water, and it makes you feel all stupid and silly."

So *that* was the explanation. Those bastards. They'd fed her Allocaine. Those sonsofbitches. To a ten-year-old. Of course. That's what it was, that's what's responsible for the picture episode—she'd had a delayed drug reaction—what do you call it, a remission, a relapse, a flashback, something like that, when the symptoms recur.

Doe shrugged. She didn't know what the stuff was called. But they had brought her to that weird house and Marie Laveau had made her speak French—

"Wait a minute. Marie who?" Something familiar struck his ear.

"Marie Laveau."

"Who's that?"

"She was this gigantic fat spade lady—"

"Black lady, Doe."

"—black lady who could only speak French, and when they gave me the stuff she picked me up—"

"What does she look like?"

"Kind of like Nina Simone. Big and fat with one of those shiny faces and scars on it, on each side." Doe ran fingers down her cheeks indicating the scars.

"Spell her name for me, can you? Her last name?"

"L-A-V-O, I guess. I don't know how she spelled it."

"Do you remember writing that name somewhere today, Doe?"

The child frowned into her dish. "Did I? On the pictures?"

Dusty looked at her critically. Was she acting? No, she barely remembered doing it. Her whole lunch period was a blur. She could recall geography at eleven, and gym at one thirty, but nothing in between. It had to be an Allocaine flashback. He would have to take her for tests, for a complete physical. He made up his mind to call Dr. Zahm the next day.

And now she was telling him all she could remember of the weirdo ceremony she'd gone through in the yard. She couldn't remember much about the first night, because she was mainly out of her head with the Allocaine, but she did remember she'd danced so hard she thought she was going to kill herself, and that was what had scared her so the second night, the idea that she'd have to dance like that again, although Mommy had promised she wouldn't, but then Mommy had made them chant, the people, and had called on someone named Sam or something, and then she'd danced in flaming gasoline!

"Yeah, that's where I came in. Tell me, what was the point of all this?"

"I don't know. But they were gonna make me do it four more nights."

"And they were only paying you scale? Who got you that booking?" Now he saw. It was simple. They'd been trying to throw a scare into the kid. Maricot had probably set Raoul up as the heavy, and when she had the kid frightened shitless she'd be the avenging angel who came and rescued Dorothy. Then Doe would want to stay with her. Well, it was over. But there were still the drug side effects to deal with. He would definitely call Dr. Zahm.

"By the way, you still want to have a funeral service for Mommy?"

"Could we, Frankie?" she asked tremulously.

"Sure, honey. I have an appointment with Father Flemyng tomorrow. I'll set it up. And you, you lucky sonofagun, you get to skip half a day of school."

"How come?"

Walking home, he told her about Dr. Parks—how it was kind of something extra Dalton had, a man you could talk to about anything, and a man who might tell you some things about yourself you never knew. He gave her the address and made a note to call Parks in the morning and tell him about Dorothy's drug experience.

"I did a picture of Frankie—that's my father—in the mountains, doing his act." Whenever she had to do a picture or write a theme, it was always about Frankie. I love him so much, she thought, I really do, but he has to stop telling people things about me. And don't forget—he killed M—— NO!!! She fought the thought, would not allow it into her consciousness, stuffed it back into whatever foul, smelly depths it came from—no, no, no, no, NO.

"NO!" And there it was, escaped, let out, the thought (he killed Mommy) hideous and quivering, lying spread out on a table all through the room, this pleasant doctor's office, with the door open to the little sun-filled garden, and in here the odor of festering honeysuckle, its cloying, palpable presence lingering like slime. The thought stood and flexed its muscles like a malevolently proud athlete, its crotch bulging sexually, obscenely, and Dorothy knew she would never feel the same about Frankie again. He killed Mommy. It wasn't his fault, but he did it.

Doctor Parks was taking it down on his pad. He had struck something here. " 'No' what, Dorothy?"

She shook her head. Under her hand she could feel the dog tensing. A long minute went by. Finally, the doctor spoke.

"If you let me in on it, I'll help you deal with it."

Up yours, doc, she thought. Stay out of it. This is between me and Frankie.

She sat in silence for a long time. Finally the doctor got up from his chair, went to the other end of the room, and brought back the five drawings from the art exhibit. The drawings she had defaced. He was going to put her through this number, he was going to attack her. Instinctively, she clutched the handle of the cha-cha. In the past two days, ever since Mommy died, she seemed to need it more, it seemed to be necessary to her in a way it had never been before. From now on she was never going to be without it.

"What is that, Dorothy?"

"My cha-cha." She shook it once, and the bones rattled inside the calabash. "I've had it since I was a kid." She noticed the Vizsla stir restlessly. His ears were up and alert.

"Do you always keep it with you?"

"Yes. It's my security blanket. Like Linus."

The doctor spread the five drawings out on the floor in front of Dorothy's chair. He sat heavily on the rug. "Dorothy, if you will, please, I'd like you to tell me about these pictures, all right? Let's start with this one." He put his hand lightly on top of the drawing of Maricot holding the machete and looking, looking, staring commandingly into Dorothy's eyes *(Je suis la bête)*. Dorothy felt the drawing move toward her (why had she shaken the cha-cha?) and Maricot's face was zooming into her eyes like a fast close-up in a movie (*Je vis dans ton coeur*) and what she was saying was, It's up to you, lahv, I'm gone now so it's up to you, *it's ahp to you*. Do it soon, do it soon, it's ahp to you—

The Vizsla snapped suddenly at Dorothy's hand, leaped up and raced wildly into the garden, out of the room. It crouched fearfully on the pebbled ground, snarling agitation and fear. The temperature in the room was suddenly freezing cold.

Dorothy whipped her hand to her mouth and began sucking it.

"Don't do that!" Doctor Parks was on his feet, tearing her hand from her mouth. "You must never suck a bite like that!" he cried, yanking her out of her chair. He led her into a small, half bathroom and washed her hand with soap and water. Fortunately, the dog's fangs hadn't broken the skin, but there were four ugly reddish indentations in the soft flesh of Dorothy's hand.

"I don't know what got into Plier," the doctor muttered. "He's never bitten anybody." He dried the hand with a small towel abstractedly.

"I think I better go to school now, Doctor Parks." The doctor nodded. He had seen enough to reach a conclusion: the child must begin therapy immediately.

21

Dusty was on his way from Forty-eighth Street to Leonard's office on Fifty-first. He had just come from the Actors' Chapel, where Father Flemyng had received him with friendliness and concern. The father had even met Maricot once, which made it more personal, nicer. Dorothy would be able to feel that Maricot was being shepherded on her final journey by a friend.

Father Flemyng had told him it would take no longer than thirty-five or forty minutes. He would offer the Eucharist, read from the scriptures, and, if Dorothy would like, there could even be an organist. They could do it any morning at ten. Father, Dusty had asked, would it be possible to do it after school hours like five o'clock? Father Flemyng had said certainly.

He barged past Mrs. Seltzer and into Leonard's office. He was lucky—Leonard was actually hanging up the phone, something he rarely did. The agent looked at him with soft-boiled eyes, filled, it seemed, with eternal aggravation. "Homowack and Stevensville. Tonight and tomorrow. I called you yesterday."

"Yeah, I know," Dusty said. "You couldn't get me

Homowack and the Nevele, could you? Always gotta make it hard for me."

"Gedahdah heah," said Leonard, and Dusty did, though pausing to give Mrs. Seltzer a wet kiss on the way out. He wondered if Leonard still made it with her. Balling Mrs. Seltzer would be classified as a mercy fuck.

He was happy about the weekend's work, even though the Stevensville was thirty miles from the Homowack, which meant considerable commuting. But he was lucky, he had wheels. Acts without wheels often had to pay busboys ten bucks to be driven from their Friday gig to their Saturday one.

He stopped by the apartment and threw a change of clothes into his overnight case. He did the same for Dorothy—an extra T-shirt, her yellow dress for evening, and her brush and comb. He would stop by school for her and take her away for a weekend in the mountains. They could both use it, a little sunshine and fresh air (and maybe some horseback riding), after the ghastliness of the past week.

As he drove through the park he thought it was a good thing some money was finally coming in, he had deliberately ignored Frank Hauser's message because he had nothing to tell him. Gee, Frank, no, I don't know when I can pay you the rest of the bread or replace your busted Sony. With the five hundred he was making this weekend he could at least give Frank something.

Then there was Paul Cobb. He had put the credit card in an envelope and sent it back with an explanatory letter itemizing what he had spent, and thanking Paul sincerely, letting him in on the whole drama of Dorothy's kidnapping, and how much it meant to have her back, and how he couldn't have done it without Paul's help. He would send Paul fifty bucks. He had signed the letter 'Irv' just in case Paul was thinking of charging him with assault and theft. Someday he'd stop back at The Painted Pony and see if he couldn't find Paul, thank him personally.

He pulled into Eighty-ninth Street and was surprised to see two squad cars, lights spinning red, and an ambulance, by the school. An officer was waving traffic through—he wasn't going to be able to wait for Doe as usual. He circled the block and found a space on Lexington, by a meter. He locked the car and walked hastily around the corner, anxious to know what was up. A fire? An accident in the swimming pool? The traffic cop stopped him as he tried to go in.

"I'm a parent of one of the kids who goes here," Dusty explained, and the cop let him through.

As he crossed the lobby frantically (had something happened to Doe?), he saw the elevator doors open, and two white-coated interns rolled out a stretcher table covered with a sheet. "Watch it . . . 'scuse please . . . coming through. . . . " Their voices had a peculiar, subdued quality that struck an eerie premonition in Dusty. It was as if these men had seen not just another accident, a concussion on a pool's edge, say, or a scalding in a shower. They sounded as if they had just seen the source of death.

Behind the interns, looking as pale as he had ever seen anyone look, was Mr. Seeger. With him was a man in a sleek St. Laurent jacket carrying a black bag—a doctor possibly? As they left the elevator the man with the bag said to Seeger, "Look, don't tell *me:* I'm telling you, my friend, nothing else leaves those particular marks."

Dusty caught Seeger by the arm. "Is Dorothy all right?"

Seeger waved him away, impatiently, which both pissed Dusty off and panicked him, simultaneously. He glanced after them, decided Seeger would be occupied for at least another five minutes, and pushed his way into the elevator, along with a bunch of older kids.

"Six," he told the elevator operator, a Chinese lady. "What happened?" The Chinese lady shrugged her shoulders in ignorance. Dusty turned to the other kids, four girls. "Does anyone know what happened?" The girls looked at him shyly and giggled. They were at that age, thirteen, fourteen. "What happened, for God's sake?" One of the girls blurted it out, and Dusty saw she wore thick steel braces on her teeth.

"One of the fourth-grade boys was in an accident."

As soon as he heard the word "boys" he felt a shock of relief run through him. He stepped off the elevator and headed for Miss Ross's homeroom, halfway down the hall. There was a knot of older kids chattering animatedly by the bulletin board as he passed, and he saw Miss Ross come out of her homeroom.

"Yeu children go heum now," she said loudly to the pack by the bulletin board. "There's neuthing more to see. Eu, helleu, Mr. Greuner." She took him by the arm and guided him into the homeroom. "We've heud a bad euccideunt today," she told him. "Eund euee theunk Deur'ty sheuld geu straight heum."

He looked around the room for Dorothy and saw her sitting very still on the green bench that ran along the opposite side of the room. There was something unnatural about her stillness, her lack of animation. As he sat down beside her, he noticed she was holding the cha-cha.

"Doe, are you okay?"

She turned to him *(Je suis la bête)* and in that instant he knew Doe had done whatever it was that had been done that day, an hour or so before, and suddenly he did not want to know what it was. There was a nameless coldness, almost a numbness (that wasn't quite it but he'd get it) in her nearly vacant stare (it was as if someone else were in there with her; Doe was doing the vacant stare but someone else was listening), and he just had to get her out of here before—before what? Before she was caught, that's what. Christ, what had she done? Whatever it was, its chill was all around them, like an aura.

"All right, come on, Doe," he said, and she allowed herself to be led out of the homeroom, into the hall, and as they stood waiting for the Chinese lady to bring up the elevator, Dusty's heart was going like sixty. I'm breakin' out, yata yata warden, slowly, slowly, into the elevator, like there's nothing wrong, and I wish she would say something, just chatter on the way she usually does, but no, she's so silent, so silent, and out into the lobby (there were new pictures on the walls) and there's Seeger and uh-oh—

"Mr. Greener." And he had to stop. It would be terribly suspicious not to speak to Seeger.

"Mr. Seeger, my God, what you must be going through."

"It's a terrible thing, terrible. The coroner just left. I'm sorry I was abrupt with you before—"

"No, no, no, not at all, I completely understand—" Though what it was he understood he did not know.

"And Dorothy must be just heartbroken. I know what good friends she was with Marvin, yesterday's ball game notwithstanding."

Marvin! So that was Marvin under the sheet. Jesus Christ, Marvin was dead?

"Does anybody have any idea, any theory? . . ." He

deliberately let his sentence trail away, waiting for Seeger to pick it up.

"How it happened?" Seeger caught his cue perfectly. "No one seems to have any idea. Fred Larrabee went into the boys' bathroom and saw him on the floor, a bloody mess. It's my private theory he slipped and cut himself on that broken sink near the window, but the coroner . . . " He shook his head dazedly, as if he could barely give credence to this next thought. " . . . The coroner says his throat was *bitten through,* as if he were attacked by a wild animal."

Dusty stole a look at Doe. She was staring straight ahead, into the lobby, emotionless, not moving. Dusty saw the lobby was filling up with Dorothy's classmates; he saw Lucy and Nicole and Sloan and Jessica—

"—nother half-assed theory," Seeger sputtered, out of character for him, but Dusty could see he was worked up about this, "which was—" Again Seeger stopped. "Never mind," he said. "I'm not about to begin parroting that idiot's dumb ideas."

"Which was what?" Dusty leaned in closer, so Seeger could whisper it sotto voce.

"Which was that those marks on Marvin's throat could only have been made by human teeth." He looked at Dusty with a disparaging expression, inviting him to join in his estimate of the coroner's ideas as being beneath consideration. Dusty heard the faint whining of a siren down the block.

"Doesn't sound too plausible, does it?"

"Of course not," Seeger snapped. He was nervously reaming out the bowl of his pipe with a small nail file. "But we'll get to the bottom of this. We're waiting for the detectives now." He swung expectantly toward the lobby windows.

"C'mon, Doe," Dusty urged her, and she started obediently forward.

"Just a minute," said Seeger authoritatively. "We've been asked to keep everybody who knew Marvin here until the detectives can talk to them."

"I'll bring her right back, Mr. Seeger, I just want to take her around the corner to the drugstore. She needs some medicine." Seeger looked doubtful, and in this moment of hesitation Dusty seized his opportunity and pushed Dorothy out the big iron doors, even as an officer approached him.

"Not supposed to leave the building," said the officer.

"We're in another grade, Officer, nothing to do with this." He took a half beat and then moved—not hurriedly, but firmly—and the officer did not stop him.

He walked hand in hand with Dorothy around the corner to Lexington. A sizable and curious crowd had been drawn by the sight of the squad cars. A delivery boy asked him what was going on, but Dusty did not answer him.

22

There was silence in the car until they crossed the Willis Avenue Bridge. Doe leaned forward and turned on the car radio. He leaned over and switched it off.

"You better talk to me, Doe. And I mean now."

She gave him a look that contained something sly and much older than she was. "What do you want to talk about, Dusty?"

That jarred him. She never called him Dusty. It was always Frankie.

"I want you to tell me about Marvin."

She studied her hands, gravely. "There's nothing to tell. You heard it all from Mr. Seeger. Freddy found him in the bathroom all bloodied up."

He swung around to look at her. She was sitting by the window, examining her hands. She seemed to be in perfect control of herself. "And where were you all this time?"

"I was around. I saw Marvin at lunch. We traded magazines."

"And after lunch?"

"I didn't see him. I was painting new pictures. That's part of my penance."

Something peculiar was going on here. Dorothy had never used the word "penance" before. "Did you just learn that word?"

She raised her left eyebrow, ever so slightly. "What, penance?" she said, and her brows made a quizzical arch. "I guess I must have."

They came to the New York Thruway and Dusty paid the first of the tolls. I must be wrong, he thought. She's perfectly composed, perfectly in control of herself. She couldn't have committed a ghastly murder just two hours ago. And the idea of Doe lacerating somebody's throat, I mean come on, who are we kidding here? Besides, she'd tell me, she's always told me everything. She wouldn't conceal something like that. Still, the ominous feeling persisted; the feeling he'd had when he first saw her, on the bench.

"You swear to me the last time you saw Marvin was at lunch?"

"Yes, I told you." Doe slapped the back of the seat. She had lost all patience. "I mean, do you think I'd be caught *dead* in the boys' bahthroom?"

She seemed to loosen up once they were in the mountains. The whole atmosphere was relaxing, there was space, trees, a lake, clean, invigorating air, and excellent food.

The show at the Homowack went fine, and Dorothy was a big hit with everybody, of course. She even got to watch the show from the spotlight and help run it. Mr. Blickstein was sorry to see her go.

"Why not stay and have lunch with us?" he said on Saturday morning.

"Thanks, Irv, we may as well get going. I promised the kid she could go horseback riding after lunch."

"Such a cowboy," Blickstein said, ruffling Dorothy's hair. "All right, we'll see you next time."

They drove the half hour to the Stevensville and unpacked. The room had two big double beds and a marvelous view of the green, gently rolling golf course. Dorothy sat on her bed, staring out the window at the grass, clutching the cha-cha.

"What is this with the cha-cha, Doe?" Lately she seemed to keep it around all the time.

"I like to have it with me."

He could understand. It was an early symbol of security; and now, especially, when the ground seemed to be shifting beneath her, he could sympathize with her need to hang on to something. Even if it was only a dopey rattle.

"You gonna take it horseback riding?" he asked.

She nodded.

It turned out there was to be no horseback riding. Very simply, the horse would not accept Doe as a rider. Pat, the riding instructor, held the horse firmly by the bridle, but each time Dorothy attempted to mount, the animal moved away with quick, agitated steps, her eyes white with fear.

"Okay, Brenda, okay there now," Pat soothed the mare. "She's just a little off her feed today, I guess." He shook his head. "Usually she's our sweetest, gentlest little girl." He gave Brenda an affectionate brush on the nose.

The mare's eyes showed white and frightened as the horse craned its neck uncontrollably. Pat was holding the horse steady. Dorothy put her foot in the stirrup for another swing atop the saddle. She gave a little preliminary hop with her ground foot, and pushed herself into midair by the stirrup. But the horse bucked away, and Doe was shaken loose from her precarious purchase and had to jump back down to the ground.

Pat steadied the horse and let the bridle go for a moment to wipe sweat from his forehead. As soon as the bridle was released, Brenda swung her huge head at Dorothy, teeth flashing. Dusty could see the pink upper lip curl dangerously, exposing the wet enamel, and the animal nipped defensively at Dorothy's head.

"Owwww," cried Doe, more in surprise than pain, and sat down with a bump. Pat immediately grabbed the bridle back.

"Hey now," said Dusty.

"I'm afraid we're going to have to retire Brenda for the afternoon," said Pat. "Let me bring out another mare, I've got a good little girl, we call her Marzipan."

"No, that's all right," Dorothy announced suddenly. "I've changed my mind." She looked at Dusty. "I think I'd rather play tennis anyway." She had just remembered

Plier, Dr. Parks's Vizsla, and somehow she knew Marzipan would not accept her either.

Something was very wrong, Dorothy knew, as she and Dusty trudged back to the main house. Animals had never been frightened of her before, they always loved her. And at that moment she felt the force inside her. She realized with a shock that the force had been there ever since Wednesday night, just kind of . . . lurking, sometimes idling, like a car engine, and at other times . . . acting. It was hard to explain, but there was one thing she knew: she didn't like it. It made her think funny, nasty somehow, and the first real indication was this thing with the animals. But hadn't there been, wasn't there something else too? The pictures at school, and, um, what about, what about . . . who? Somebody she'd hurt really bad, I mean *really* bad . . . had killed, in fact. Hadn't she? In a place that had two stalls with black doors on them, and three urinals, and a broken sink . . . she wanted to tell someone, but she didn't know how to explain it so it wouldn't sound crazy, so somebody would believe her and not just think she had to go to Dr. Parks. And then she was conscious of the force inside her (*Je suis la bête*) revving up just a little beyond the idling stage, and she had to pay close attention—now that she'd defined it for herself she knew how to recognize it and the force was saying, no, not saying in so many words, but making her feel it, telling her to relax, don't sweat it, just go with it, I'm here when you need me. *Je vis dans ton coeur.*

The tennis pro was named Kathy, and she gave Dorothy quite a workout. Dorothy insisted Dusty play, too, and Dusty was embarrassed at not being much good; Doe could tell he didn't like taking lessons from a girl.

"Keep your arm level and follow through," Kathy told them, and Doe got used to it quite quickly. At the end of an hour she was able to get the ball back over the net about 40 percent of the time.

They stayed on the court for an extra hour after Kathy had to leave to teach someone else. When they got back to their room, Dusty motioned her to the bathroom. "You take the first shower, hon."

She went into the bathroom before she stripped off her T-shirt. She was just beginning to get breasts, and she was starting to feel self-conscious about undressing in front of him. "Can we do it again tomorrow, Frankie? I love it!"

"Sure, sweetheart." He was so glad she was calling him Frankie again. She seemed to be coming out of whatever funk she'd been in yesterday. He wondered what he was going to say to Seeger on Monday, how to explain his abduction of Dorothy. He'd called the service last night, after the show, and, sure enough, there had been a call from Seeger. He stretched out on the bed, his legs aching from chasing the ball around the court.

"You know what I could go for right now?" he yelled into the bathroom. "A steambath and a massage."

"They've got 'em here, Frankie. There's a sauna, and a guy who gives massages, a masseur. That's for you. They have to have a masseuse for me, 'cause I'm a girl. Mommy taught me that. Never take a massage from a masseur, make sure it's a masseuse."

Dusty heard the shower go on, and emotion welled in his throat. She had actually been able to refer to Maricot naturally, without thinking, with no bad reaction. She was gonna be all right, maybe, hunh? Please, please, let her be all right.

Doe brought the cha-cha to rehearsal, and Mace, the drummer, who was always throwing lines, asked her did she have her union card, because, you know, cutie, there's only room for one percussionist in this hotel. Doe giggled, and even blushed a little (Dusty remembered the girls in the Dalton elevator). She was getting to that stage. Dusty would have to keep his eyes open. From now on it was gonna be boys, boys, boys.

And in the middle of dinner Doe did a little hoochy-kooch dance. It happened when Mace rolled up his sleeve, and on his arm was a tattoo of a mermaid. Mace had been in the Navy, and had learned how to make the mermaid dance, and he did it for Doe, he flexed his biceps, and the place where the fishtail joined the girl's torso wiggled up and down obscenely, except it was cute on Mace.

And suddenly Dorothy was up and lifting her yellow dress above her waistline and rippling her belly muscles in exactly the same way, so that if there had been a drawing on her tummy—a face, say—the face would've gone into funny expressions.

Mace sang, "Da da *daaah* da *daaah*, da da dadee dadee *daaah*," and everybody laughed, and Dusty thought, Yeah, maybe I can let myself feel better about her.

At showtime Dorothy disappeared, and he lost track of her for two hours. She caught up with him in the coffee shop, about one o'clock in the morning. "Hey, Doe, you want some German chocolate cake? It's dynamite."

"No, I'm tryna lose weight. Thin is in, you know."

"Well get *you,*" he said to her, and all the Feinsteins laughed.

They got back to the room and Doe put the cha-cha under her pillow. "Guess who I sat with tonight?" she asked him.

"Animal, vegetable, or mineral?" He was stripping off his ruffled blue tux shirt.

"Come on, guess."

"Rick Blaine," he said. "Know who that is?"

"Shure, shweethaht," she said, doing it very well, too, "I know who Rick Blaine ish, and it washn't him shee? It was Thorpe, the Mass Sewer." She broke herself up with this.

"Who?"

"I sat with the Mass Sewer, and he promised to introduce me to the Mass Soooss. He said she was Dr. Seuss's son by a previous marriage." She started rolling all over the room. Dusty looked at her with amusement. "Doe, did somebody feed you wine or something?"

"Yes!" she blurted. "Thorpe, the Mass Sewer." She broke into fresh snorts of laughter. "He said anytime you want to come in, just bring me and he'll give us a special rate. The Sewer Rate." She chortled and flopped on the bed. "Gee, I thought I'd bounce off," she said, lying, panting, face down on the acrylic spread. "I thought this was a trampoline. I guess it's just a bed." She rolled herself off and fell to the floor with a clunk, where she lay emitting a series of short barks.

"Yurp, yurp, yurp," she cried, and flapped the backs of her hands together. She inched herself on her belly and elbows to the luggage stand, where Dusty stood folding his pants into his suitcase. She nuzzled his ankle with her nose and cried, "Yurp, yurp, yurp!"

"What're you, a seal?"

"I'm a Christmas seal," she said. "I'm the Good Housekeeping Seal."

"You want me to book you into the zoo? There's an opening."

"Are you giving this seal the Seal of Approval?"

"Get up, schmucko." The minute the words were out of his mouth he was sorry. It had been a long time since she'd had this kind of silly fun, and it would be a shame to throw cold water on it. But she stayed on her belly all the way into the bathroom, and he heard her brushing her teeth in rhythm. I should feed her half a bottle of wine with her dinner now and then, he ruminated. Good for what ails you.

During the night he had a very sexy dream. He dreamed Maricot was going down on him, slide, lick, sliiiide, liiiick, and as his cock disappeared into her soft wet lips it was just like it used to be, she was devouring him, sucking all of him up into her beautiful deep mouth, sliiide, liiiick, and pause, curl the tongue around it, flick the ridge of his cock tantalizingly slowly, see the bright string of saliva bridging her lip and his cock, and bigger, swelling, throbbing, Oh, Christ, this is it, I can't hold it anymore, here I go, and his cock grew thicker, it was immense, forcing her cheeks out, and as he shot she withdrew her mouth and looked straight into his eyes with this terrifying, triumphant stare, a stare of the utmost evil, and he looked down at his cock and he was coming blood!

He woke up clutching his groin and lay with his hands there, his heart pounding, until he was clear enough to assure himself he was all right. Damn. What a terrific dream. Till the end, anyway. He hadn't actually come in his sleep, but damn near, damn near. It would've been the first wet dream he'd had since he was fifteen.

He looked over at Doe's bed, and it was empty, and freshly made up. Ah, what a good kid. Saving the maid work. He could tell by the light under the drape it was somewhere around mid-morning. He looked at his watch: ten past eleven. Too late for breakfast, but Marcy the waitress would sneak him some juice and coffee. That would hold him till lunch.

He got up to go into the bathroom, and as he passed Doe's bed he saw a design drawn in the nap of the carpet between the bed and the wall. Straddling it between his feet, he sat on her bed and examined it more closely. It was the same design she had drawn on Lucy Gross's picture of the rabbit and the giraffe—a rectangle with a cross above it. As he sat there, he had that same, undefinable queasy feeling of . . . of coffins and tombs that he had felt so strongly in Seeger's office on Thursday.

He went into the bathroom. As he showered he made up his mind to ask Doe about the cross and the tomb. Maybe she better spend a few afternoons with Doctor Parks after all.

He still didn't like getting tennis lessons from a girl. But it was making Doe happy, so he ran around in the bright Sunday-afternoon sunshine and let Kathy correct his swing and his serve and his backhand. But about quarter to five, he had had all he could take.

"That's enough for me. You girls want to continue, you go ahead." On the court, the shadow of the net had lengthened to about twelve feet.

"I think this little one's had enough, too," said Kathy. "She's about ready to take on Chrissy Everts, aren't you, Dorothy?"

Doe squinted up at Kathy gratefully. "Okay, now we have to go and visit Thorpe," she chirped. "I promised him."

"You told me who Thorpe is, but I forgot."

"Doncha remember? He's the Mass—" Dodo grinned mischievously, waiting for Dusty to cut her off before she said "sewer."

"Oh, yeah, your drinking buddy."

"He's really very good," said Kathy. "I know people who come here just for him. You really feel sensational after Thorpe gets through with you."

"C'mon, Frankie. He's right around here, behind the kitchen."

"Enjoy yourselves, you two," said Kathy.

Thorpe was picking up towels and tossing them into a big rolling canvas wagon when they stepped into his domain. He was about forty-five, dressed all in white—white T-shirt, white jeans, white sneakers. When he saw Dorothy, he crouched down on his haunches and stretched out his arms. She ran full-tilt into them, and Thorpe picked her up. Dusty advanced slowly into the room, feeling the wetness and the heat seeping into him.

"Frankie, this is Thorpe."

"And this is my liddle chambion," said Thorpe. He iss chust a liddle pit Cherman, thought Dusty.

"Hello, Mr. Thorpe. Thanks for looking after Dorothy last night. She came home drunk as a skunk."

Dorothy laughed shyly. Thorpe still held her in his massive arms.

"Ja, ve had a liddle schnapps together, didn't ve, chamb?"

Dorothy giggled some more. Oh, yes, it was starting. The boys, the boys. That's why Dorothy was fascinated by Thorpe. The muscles, the physicality.

"And you, you are a funny man," Thorpe said to Dusty.

"You're from Germany?" Dusty inquired.

Thorpe smiled. "Switzerland. I am from Lausanne."

Sure, thought Dusty, and I'm from Mars. That's what you tell all the girls, I'll bet. It woudn't be kosher to have a German masseur in a Jewish resort hotel. Still, the guy must be damn good to get past his accent.

Thorpe set Dorothy down. "Come, Mr. Greener," he said. "I give you massage. I give you massage you don't forget." He wheeled two long, rectangular padded tables into the center of the room. Down the hall Dusty could see the doors to the saunas; they were of that dark, reddish wood, with thick glass windows in them.

"Me too?" Doe asked.

"Ja, you too, chamb." He looked at the big white clock on the wall. "Nopody comes down now, ve put the poys and girls togezzer, lige Adam and Eve. If you vould lige to change in brivate, ve haf a room." He indicated the changing room with a large, capable-looking hand.

"Okay, Doe, you go in there."

"Moment," said Thorpe, and crossed to an open locker in which were stacked a pile of clean white towels. He flicked one expertly across the room to Doe, and she went inside. Dusty began taking off his clothes. "Dot one is a liddle terror," said Thorpe.

"Absolutely horrifying," Dusty agreed. He tried to slip his sweaty Lacoste shirt over his head, but it caught on his shoulders and he had to grunt it off. He was sticky from the tennis.

"You know, she told me she wants to pe a gomig, chust lige her father."

"No kidding?" She had mentioned it once or twice, but he never believed she was serious about it. So she'd told Thorpe that was her ambition. Well, he'd talk her out of *that*. Showbiz was no place for anyone, especially Dorothy, with all her other aptitudes. He took off his sneakers and socks, and the smell embarrassed him.

"I think I'd like a shower," he said to Thorpe.

"Ja, certainly." The burly masseur led him down the hall. Opposite the saunas was a room roughly twelve feet square with three shower nozzles on the far wall. Dusty turned on the middle one, adjusted the handle for temperature, and gratefully felt the water steam down his back. He soaped himself all over, and when he had scrubbed his armpits, groin, and toes clean from sweat, he stood, head bowed like a penitent, beneath the driving water. It felt wonderful, for the moment it washed away the cares, the problems (what was he gonna say to Seeger?). Oh, later, he thought; right now I'm gonna concentrate on this.

He was standing there, luxuriating in the water when Dorothy came in. She smiled tentatively at him through the steam and turned on the shower to his left. He hadn't seen her naked for over a year, and his eyes noted the tiny spot of darkness where her legs sprouted from her torso, and the small thickenings of flesh on her chest. Her smile was friendly and open, and she didn't seem to be at all embarrassed. Gee, he thought, would that be wonderful, if she just never had to go through any embarrassment about showing her body?

He passed her the soap, and it popped out of her hand, and she laughed as she retrieved it, the shower splashing her hair into a slick brown helmet that clung to her head, and there she was, just showering and smiling, smiling in the shower.

They were lying on Thorpe's cushioned tables, towels over their butts, face down. Thorpe was kneading Dusty's fingers (he had started with the toes) pulling them out, one by one, rolling them around in his grip. Dusty could hear the joints giving small bony crackles.

By the table was a waist-high rolling trolley which held, in addition to skin mitts and rubbing acohol, several unmarked jars of white lotion. From time to time Thorpe would pour out a palmful of lotion, and Dusty would feel it slap down on his calves, his rump, his back, feel it being rubbed in with powerful hands.

"What is that stuff?" Doe wanted to know.

"Dot's the zecret formula. Luff botion number nine."

"Come on, what is it?"

"You vill pe very dizappoinded when I tell you. It's called Lubriderm—zey use it a grade deal in ze hospital."

Thorpe was good, all right. Deft, strong, and sensitive. His hands created relaxation from tension. Dusty soon quit analyzing the dynamic of the massage and abandoned himself to the wonderful limp dumbness of just pouring his face into the headrest, his limbs almost weightless, or maybe so weighty he couldn't feel them (if that made any sense), arms dangling, the clean, antiseptic scent of the Lubriderm almost giving him a high. . . .

Thorpe was doing Doe now, he could hear the slap and pummel of his hands on her firm young flesh. I'll bet that horny Kraut is really getting off on this, he thought, but without resentment—he was feeling much too relaxed to do anything but smile—and then the sounds stopped and he sensed Thorpe cross to the other end of the room. Doe's voice wafted over to him.

"You like it, Frankie?"

" 'S terrific, doncha think, hon?"

"I love it, I love it, I *love* it."

Where was she getting the energy, he wondered.

"I durn on ze steam," Thorpe was saying, "und zen, vhen I finish, you can lie here, long as you lige, and no von vill pozzer you, ja?" He gave Doe a final once-over, from neck to toes, with his magic fingers.

Doe's tone was dreamy. "I feel like I'm made out of rubber," she murmured.

"Hey, Thorpe." Dusty sighed, his eyes nearly closed. "You wanna go on the road?"

"Ja, und vot vould ze Ztevenzville do?"

Cable Lausanne for another, Dusty wanted to say, but Thorpe would not have thought it was funny.

There was silence for a long time. Dusty drowsed in and out of consciousness. Then he heard a soft rattley sound and the next thing he knew, fingers were on the inside of his right leg, behind the knee. Little tickley fingers making designs, it felt like figure eights perhaps, on the back of his leg. It felt delicious. Who's doing that? He had the feeling Thorpe was gone, so it must be someone else, drawing figure eights in the Lubriderm behind his knees, and now the little fingers were sliding up the backs of his thighs, and he turned over to look, but slowly, not to break the delicious drowsiness of the relaxation, and now her fingers were on the tops of his thighs and she was smiling at him all kind of open and not embarrassed at all—

"Jahst relahx lahv," she said, and the steam—he could feel it now, lulling him, a fine fizz of moisture in his eyes. Oh, God, this is so good, I could stay like this for about eight zillion years . . . what had she asked him?

"Whadja say, darling?" his eyes were half closed, his voice carried no energy whatever. "I said 'jahst relahx.'" And in her eyes he saw those other eyes, yes, deep in there, hidden and smiling and so beautiful, so very beautiful, and her face came toward him. She brought her hands up, brushing the towel away, over his hipbone, resting lightly just inches from his penis, and now her mouth was close to his, and he lay there helpless, and she grazed his cheek with her own, he felt her lashes brush his nose, he was bringing her mouth just above his, and then she licked him, on the lips, and he closed his eyes, and, oh, Lord, she was putting her tongue in his mouth, so warm, warm and expert, and terribly, terribly sexy. He bit down on it very lightly, the way she liked him to, and he heard her give a throaty little chuckle of pleasure and he simply lay there and let her do all the work, the way she sometimes liked to, he remembered his dream this morning. Oh, yes, soon she'd take him in her mouth, and then he felt the skin on his penis stretching, the little moist sweaty areas drying quickly, and now she was taking tiny little nips from his chest, from his nipples with her teeth, oh, delicious, and her hand moved deliberately across him and the fingers encircled him and began gently slipping up and down, up and down, Oh, God, what heaven, what a heavenly trip, and now he opened his eyes, and she was looking at him with the knowledge of a billion years, with woman's primal, eternal knowledge. Oh, Christ, the most desirable, the sexiest, the most powerful, stimulating. . . . Wait, wait a minute, something's wrong, *something is very wrong,* this is not Maricot!

"Stop it, Doe."

She looked up, surprised. He had not moved, but his eyes were awake now. Her hand was still around his cock. She did not take it away.

"Am I doing it wrong?" she said, and in that moment, in that crazy, emotionally crossed feedback instant Dusty knew his child was in the grip of something unspeakably evil. He had tried to dismiss it before, not to see it, to repress it, shove it back down into the grim abyss from which it came, but it had pushed out, like intestines from a ripped belly, to cover his child, cover her in an obscenity, an obscenity they would have to fight.

He leaped off the table. "Get dressed!" he yelled at her. "We're going home!" He saw the surprise in the child's face and grieved for her. She did not know what was happening to her. He truly believed she was an innocent, and that she could be saved.

23

In the Volvo, speeding south on the Henry Hudson Parkway, he pressed her about the meaning of the cross and the tomb.

"What do you mean you don't know? You drew it."

"It's just a drawing, Frankie."

"And that's another thing: what's my name these days, Frankie, Dusty, Daddy, or what?"

"What do you mean?"

"In the past three days you've called me all those names, now I wanna know why. You called me 'lahv,' too, the way Mommy did. Now I wanna know *what's going on!*"

Dorothy was scared to be in the car with him—his driving was erratic and unpredictable. Twice he had almost careened into the toll booths.

"Frankie, slow down."

"When you tell me what I wanna know I'll slow down, okay?" He deliberately floored the accelerator. The car sprinted to seventy-five.

"Frankie! Slow down! Please!"

"What happened to Marvin Berman?"

"I don't know."

"Bullshit. You know plenty." He kicked the car up to eighty.

Doe cowered away from him, over by the door. Was he gonna kill them both?

"What happened to Marvin Berman?"

"Frankie! All I remember is seeing him on the floor! That's all! I don't remember anything else—how I got in the bathroom or anything! That's the truth!"

"All right, now we're getting somewhere." He slowed the car to sixty. "Just tell me what you remember."

She kept her eyes on the speedometer. "I just remember I saw him at lunch, and we traded magazines, and I told him he better not clip me anymore in basketball."

"And what did he say?" Doe didn't answer. "What did he say, Doe?"

Doe's lip curled into a menacing sneer. "He said, 'Up your giggy, Mung-face.' " She gave a snort of satisfaction.

"So then?"

"So then I kept an eye on him. We had the same study period. And when I saw him raise his hand and Miss T excused him, I snuck out." Her eyes gleamed with anticipation now, with an unhealthy, dreamy glimmer.

"And?"

"And then he went in the bathroom (yes, she remembered this now) and I went in right after and hid in one of the booths, and while he was peeing—" She looked around wildly. "The cha-cha!" she cried, in great agitation. "Where's the cha-cha?"

"I packed it, Doe, relax." Something funny was going on with that cha-cha. Maybe he should wean her away from it. God, she was strange—like another person. "So finish," he said. The dreamy glimmer returned to her eyes. It was like she was slipping in and out of her own character, it was really schizzy.

"—by the sink," she was saying. "And he laughed, 'cause I was in the boys' bathroom. And I said, 'Take back calling me Mung-face,' and he just laughed harder. So, I . . . " She stopped.

"What?"

"I killed him, lahv," she said simply, except it wasn't simple at all. Maricot appeared behind her eyes in a flash so intensely frightening he swerved the car and almost hit a Buick on his right. It was as if Maricot's face had been superimposed on Doe's—no, that wasn't it, it was as if

Maricot was actually *inside* Doe's head, peering out through her eyes.

Whatever this evil was, it had something to do with Maricot. Whatever had been done to Doe last week in the bayous of Louisiana had been Maricot's doing. I'll go back there, he thought, get hold of this Marie Lavo person, whoever she is, and find out exactly what Maricot did to cause this, this double identity, this malevolent schizophrenia.

They were upstairs now, and Doe unpacked her case, and then she murmured something about going over to Gina's for a moment, and he said okay and went into the bedroom and sat on the foot of the bed.

Maybe he should call Dr. Parks. Yes, now, right now, at eight forty-five Sunday evening, before it got any worse. He stared down at his boots, pondering it. Still, you know, it could very well be that fuckin' Allocaine. He had heard of those relapse flashback things happening as long as a year afterward, people walking off roofs and out into the middle of freeways, and the hell with Dr. Zahm, I'm taking that kid to Johns Hopkins, goddamn it, let 'em put her through the mill, see if there's still traces of that junk in her bloodstream, and oh, if that cunt weren't already dead I'd kill her now. How dare she, how *dare* she mess around with the kid's head like that, and he heard the door close softly and Doe's steps in the kitchen. And meanwhile (he almost laughed, it was so painful) the kid's facing a charge of murder one. I don't believe it, she didn't do that, she *didn't,* she couldn't have. And yet there it was, there it was, and he lay down on the bed looking up. Oh, God, why did you let this happen, why the kid? why such an arbitrary . . . and the old line ran through his head, "*'cause you piss me off,*" and he had to laugh because if he didn't laugh he would have to weep, and he heard her close the door of the fridge and something so tender and protective welled up in him, and he shifted over onto his belly and reached for a Kleenex on the night table because he couldn't help it now, he was crying, crying for Doe, for that hateful destruction Maricot had wreaked on her, for the loss of innocence— It was like a car after a crash—you could fix it but it would never be the same.

Doe came into the darkened bedroom with a glass in her hand. "Look what I found at Gina's," she said, hand-ing it to him. He tasted it. It was wine, dry and sunny; probably Italian.

"Verdicchio?"

"Soave," she said, and noticed the Kleenex crushed in his hand. "Are you okay?"

He gave a small sigh. "I'm worried about you."

"I'll be okay." She yanked at the sleeve of his jacket. "C'mon, take this off." She helped him wriggle out of it, and then placed the two bed pillows behind him and pushed him back on them.

"What's this, your Marcus Welby impression?"

"I'm lucky to have a daddy that worries about me. A lot of the kids' folks just leave them with people." She was tugging at his boot. He raised his foot just high enough to allow her to slip it off. He took a long sip of the Soave. Oh, yes, he could certainly use a glass or two of this.

"Okay, Frankie, I've got a surprise performance for you, okay? You just relax and stay right there, okay?" She disappeared into the living room. He smiled ruefully. When she was five and six she had put on shows for them—him and Maricot. She would write her own scripts, little plays and sketches. She did one once that used all his impressions. She had studied his tapes and learned everybody—Cagney, John Wayne, everybody. He shook his head. Those days were gone forever.

Dorothy came into the shadowed bedroom with a cylindrical shaker of Gold Medal flour and a large conga drum, which she must've gotten at Gina's, 'cause there was no such item around here.

"You gonna do a show for me?"

"Unh-hunh. I'm gonna show you what Mommy did in Louisiana; I remembered it all in the car."

His smile was grim with satisfaction. Okay, he told himself. Now we'll see what's going on here. He settled back on the pillows.

"Listen, did you manage to con Gina out of the whole bottle?"

"Sure." She dashed into the kitchen, and he heard the fridge open and close. When she came back she was carrying the tall green bottle, which she handed him. He noticed her other hand held the cha-cha and a can of lighter fluid.

"What's that for?"

"Oh, listen, if we want him to appear, I have to dance in fire."

"Want who to appear?"

"Baron Samedi."

"Who the hell is Baron Samedi?"

"Oh, Dusty," she said. "Don't you know anything?" She smiled at him teasingly. "He's the God of the Dead."

"No kidding."

"Sure," she said, and stood ceremoniously at the foot of the bed. "In fact this whole program was made possible by a grant from The Dead. Bread from the Dead."

Funny, he thought. She *could* be a comic, come to think of it, and a good one. Her instincts and timing were marvelous. She was bringing him the drum, placing it horizontally on top of him between his legs.

"Okay," she said, "now what I have to do is play the cha-cha, and you have to keep time on the drum, okay? And you can't ever stop, or he won't come, y'understand?"

"I understand. Where do you want it, about here?" He snapped his fingers a few times, to establish the count.

"Unh-hunh." He started beating the tempo—it was easy enough, one, two, three, four, ah-one, ah-two, ah-three, ah-four, Lawrence Welk time.

" 'Kay, now you have to say, *'Fait un vever pou moin'* over and over again, okay? In time with the drum."

"Listen, who's doing this show, you or me?"

"C'mon, start."

And he took a final swallow and put the wine down and started. One, two, three, four, *fettun vevey poo mwah,* three, four, *fettun vevey poo mwah,* three, four, and she was sprinkling flour from the shaker to the floor, and what was she drawing?

"Baron Samedi," she whispered in the dark bedroom. "I invoke you, I draw your symbol, I make this vever for you, great Ghêde, Lord of the Dead, Baron Cimitière, Baron Samedi." She shook the cha-cha once, and Dusty heard the rattle of the bones, and he leaned forward to see, and she had drawn the cross over the tomb, and then a circle of flour around the drawing and she looked up at him from the floor and then she said "How do you like me so far?" and he very nearly broke up but he didn't want to interrupt his chanting, three, four, *fettun vevey poo mwah,* three, four, and now she was pouring lighter fluid on the circle of flour, and oh, no, she's lighting it up, and he wanted to tell her don't burn the place down but he was fascinated, almost mesmerized by his own drumming and chanting—once you got caught up in it you want to keep going—and now she was talking again—

"Baron Samedi, I call upon you, I offer proof of my devotion, the dance of fire, I am a true canzo, accept me, hear me, attend me."

And she's dancing in the fuckin' fire, and this is the damnedest thing, as the fire burns higher the room is getting colder. How is that possible? And he saw her take the chef's knife, the one she cut the carrots with, and slowly push it into her belly and he wanted to stop her, but somehow he could not take his hands from the drum, and there was a new quality to her voice now—

"I do not call you lightly, Baron Samedi, I am prepared to withstand ahgonizing pain."

Something shiny and evil appeared in Dorothy's face. This wasn't a game anymore. Maricot was in there again, this is a trick, a plot, and now Dorothy was dancing by the foot of the bed, and when she spoke her voice was Maricot's, and come on, let's quit it now, but try as he might he could not take his hands from the drum, and this creature—it wasn't Dorothy anymore—it was something half human and doing jokes. Dahsty, you oughta be on the stage. There's one leaving in five minutes. Oh, no, the oldest line in the world, and the burning flour was acrid in his nostrils. I know you're out there, Dahsty, I cahn hear you breathing, and she's throwing these rotten old Morty Storm lines and coming around the bed. You weren't born here, Dahsty, but you're dying here and that one struck a terrifying nerve. Yes, that one hurt. She's getting closer. The eyes, the eyes are Satanic, oh, Christ. And a bum came up to me and said I haven't had a bite in days so I bit him—

And she lunged for his throat, clamping her teeth into his esophagus, and he knew this was no show, she *meant to kill him,* and he tried to tear away but she held on, and he could feel her sharp incisors crunching through his Adam's apple, and he was coughing and the burned sugar smell gave way to the copper taste of his own blood as he saw a great spout of it leap across the bedspread, and he wrenched himself over to the right and the drum fell on the floor, and, Christ, she's *coming with me,* hanging on by her teeth, her eyes holding a glittering menace, and he rammed the palms of his hands into her shoulders and felt the searing agony in his throat and still she hung on, and finally he took his right fist and drew it back under him and uppercut her hard in the temple and her mouth relaxed for an instant as the blow stunned her, and he was able to draw away and suck in a breath and as he did he heard the awful burble of air bubbling into his neck through his own blood, and he was off and around the bed, but she threw herself in front of the door, and he could feel the message beaming from those fierce, glittering eyes. I'm going to kill you, you're going to die, and this isn't schizophrenia, that's *Maricot* in there. And as he tried to leap over her at the door, she grabbed with both hands at crotch level, and suddenly she had him down and in her viselike little hands. Christ, where does she get this strength? *Oowww,* God, she's breaking my nuts and there in her mouth, oh, Jesus, I can see the flesh from my throat, I can even see my beard on the skin and the purple gouts of dark blood. The pain in his groin was so excruciating he knew he would have to pass out, and then somehow he felt something bang his shoulder and it was the drum and he reached behind his head while the agony built in his balls (she was about to bite him there, he could see the glittering eyes devour him there) and he brought the big wooden cylinder above his head and crashed it down upon her as hard as he possibly could—

Her face rocketed back in surprised anger. He had struck her on the forehead, and though he could see a deep gash, there was *no blood,* and in the living room he heard the étagère topple over, though they were nowhere near it, and it still wasn't stopping her. He saw the red mouth snarl open and the gleaming-edged teeth covered with *his flesh,* and she was something unearthly and obscene and the message came very strongly. She didn't say anything, she lasered it to him from her mind, You will be dead in three minutes. I'm going to kill you. And she raised herself on her arms and gathered her legs under her to spring once more at his throat and he half sat up and bounced his butt back into the bedroom through the cauterized flour and lighter fluid and his palm fell upon the handle of the chef's knife and as she lunged at him, open jawed, he brought the knife up to chest level with both fists, and she saw it there but she had started her spring, it was too late to stop. She didn't even have time to close her mouth, and she swallowed the blade, impaled herself on it, and Dusty heard the scream in his mind as he concentrated on holding the handle steady—he heard the crunch of cartilage and the solid *thunk* of bone against the point, and suddenly the blade of the knife glowed orange and then yellow and then white, as if the carbon were being tempered again, with heat from another world, and for a moment she hung there, skewered, and then her body dropped, inert, to his chest but her eyes were still staring into his, hungry for him, for his life, and he saw blood well out of her nostrils, ears, mouth, and the blood was boiling, literally boiling with tiny bubbles that spattered his face as they popped, and he was transfixed so in horror by the bulging face staring at him that it was half a minute before he realized he would have to let go of the knife before her head could fall, and then he did, and her head fell forward, the knife handle protruding from her mouth like some huge tongue depressor and the boiling blood was flooding his sweater and he pushed her frantically off and ringing him where he half sat, half lay the circle of flour, burning with a fearfully intense white flame and there was a dreadful keening in his ears, louder and louder, as if all the souls in purgatory were screaming at him, and as he watched in terror Doe's body began to heave and shudder, filling itself as if from an unseen bellows, like some kind of horrible blowfish, until he knew it had to burst and he thought he saw, he couldn't be sure, he would tell the police later it was a hallucination but the thing's face (it wasn't Dorothy, it wasn't even human) rose and grinned at him once, hideously, and simultaneously he heard a deafening detonation, an explosion that rocked the building, he was thrown again to the floor and he saw little white fragments of bone spatter the walls and ceiling and he realized the cha-cha had exploded and the room was filled with the nauseating stench of death, and he could hear people in the hall outside opening their doors and the blowfish body was sinking to the floor now for the last time and they were pounding on his door and he rose shakily to his feet, feeling the blood throb from his throat as he tried to cross the living room, but he could only get as far as the couch before he fell to his knees, and as he sank into unconsciousness they were jimmying his door, thank God, but he knew they would never believe him.

9 781451 620870